"You and I are friends."
Jill's voice trembled.

"I want to be more than your friend," Dan said.

"But we agreed—"

"I didn't agree to anything," he interrupted. His gaze still held hers. "My feelings haven't changed. I want to see where our attraction leads us."

Denying she was attracted to him would be fruitless. Even if she hadn't already admitted as much, he might be able to tell that little goose bumps had popped up on her skin where he'd touched her.

"We've already been over this," she said, "and I'm not staying in Indigo Springs."

Dear Reader,

Almost everyone is familiar with the fable about the boy who cried wolf. In *That Runaway Summer*, Jill Jacobi's ten-year-old brother is a variation of that boy. Except when he comes to Jill with a fantastic tale others have discounted, she believes him. She even goes on the run to protect him.

Jill and her brother wind up in Indigo Springs, which may well be the end of the road for them. I know it is for me. *That Runaway Summer* is the final installment in my five-book series set in the scenic Pocono Mountain town that isn't nearly as tranquil as it looks. Then again, if it were, visiting there wouldn't be quite as interesting!

Until next time,

Darlene Gardner

P.S. Visit me on the Web at www.darlenegardner.com.

That Runaway Summer
Darlene Gardner

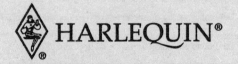

HARLEQUIN®

TORONTO • NEW YORK • LONDON
AMSTERDAM • PARIS • SYDNEY • HAMBURG
STOCKHOLM • ATHENS • TOKYO • MILAN • MADRID
PRAGUE • WARSAW • BUDAPEST • AUCKLAND

Recycling programs
for this product may
not exist in your area.

ISBN-13: 978-0-373-71666-1

THAT RUNAWAY SUMMER

ABOUT THE AUTHOR

While working as a newspaper sportswriter, Darlene Gardner realized she'd rather make up quotes than rely on an athlete to say something interesting. So she quit her job and concentrated on a fiction career that landed her at Harlequin/Silhouette Books, where she wrote for the Temptation, Duets and Intimate Moments lines before finding a home at Superromance. Please visit Darlene on the Web at www.darlenegardner.com.

Books by Darlene Gardner

HARLEQUIN SUPERROMANCE

*Return to Indigo Springs

To my parents Mary and Charles,
because their love story has lasted through
more than fifty years of marriage.

PROLOGUE

"HE'S HIRED a private investigator to track you down." Her mother's voice was breaking up, not entirely due to the scratchy reception.

A shuddering sound reverberated, so raucous it seemed to shake the cramped living room in the furnished apartment Jill Jacobi had rented six weeks ago. Her eyes flew to the door as if her pursuer would burst through any second.

But it was the air conditioner sputtering and rattling before finally blasting her face with semicool air.

"Did you hear me?" Her mother's familiar Southern drawl came over the phone, the connection clearer now. "He said if you called me I should tell you it's only a matter of time before his private investigator finds you."

Jill's knuckles showed white on the prepaid cell phone. She loosened her grip and reminded herself she could find a kernel of good in even the worst news.

He hadn't called in the cops.

"Don't worry, Mama," she said, her tone deliberately light. She parted the pretty yellow-and-white-gingham curtains she'd hung to brighten up the room and studied the Columbia, South Carolina, street below. A few cars passed by, but the businesses were closed and the sidewalks empty. No one was watching the apartment building. "A private eye can't find me."

"How do you know that, darlin'?" Her mother sounded worried, the way she had every time Jill checked in. Then again, her mother had been anxious about something or other since her divorce from Jill's father. That had been a full two decades ago when Jill was eight. "Private eyes are like bird dogs. You don't know the first thing about throwing one off a scent."

Jill was more savvy than she'd been in the last town, when she'd taken into her confidence the friendly young mother who lived next door. She'd barely escaped Savannah in time after discovering her so-called friend had tried to exchange her whereabouts for reward money.

"I know a little something about covering my tracks, Mama," Jill said. "I withdrew all the money from my bank account, I don't list my address anywhere and I don't use credit. I'm even using money orders for my car payments."

Who was she trying to reassure? Jill wondered. Her mother or herself?

"I hate that you're living this way," her mother said. "You were so happy in Atlanta. You were going to buy into that bike shop and you had all those nice friends."

"I can make friends wherever I go." Jill refused to dwell on her lost business opportunity. "I can be happy anywhere."

She wished that were true of her mother, a nurse who had long operated under the hope that the next hospital job or the next condo or the next man held the key to her happiness.

"How can you be content when you're always looking over your shoulder? That's no way to live."

"It's the way it has to be."

"No!" Her mother was probably shaking her head, the curly dark hair that was so like Jill's rustling from side to side. "No, it isn't. You can go on back to Atlanta and get your life together."

"You know I can't do that," Jill said quietly.

"Why not?" her mother demanded. "He's not a bad man."

Her mother had a point, but that didn't change the situation. "You know why. We've been over it a dozen times."

"And for the life of me I still don't understand why you're so sure this is the only way."

"Because it *is* the only way." Jill cut her off before her mother launched into what had become a familiar refrain. "Thanks for telling me about the private eye."

Silence.

"I'll be in touch when I can." Jill couldn't promise anything more specific than that. "Bye, Mama. I love you."

She rang off before her mother could say anything else, then sat down on the thin mattress of the sofa bed to assess her situation.

Even with her new ironclad policy of trusting no one, she could have unwittingly left a trail.

She hadn't seen a way around using her own Social Security number. When she'd filled out the employment papers for her waitress job, it had been with the assumption that no one but the cops could get access to her records.

Had that been naive? Private eyes on TV were always calling in favors with their law enforcement contacts. Did it work that way in real life, too?

Her eyelids finally grew heavy and she clicked off the living-room lamp with the sunflower shade she'd picked out herself. She usually had no trouble falling asleep, but tonight she felt the mattress coils poking at her ribs. Her eyes popped open at every noise.

She must have finally slept, because the weak light of dawn filtering through the shades woke her. Her mind felt clear, the indecision that had plagued her the night before gone. She didn't linger in the sofa bed, for she had much to do.

When she was almost ready, she opened the creaky door to the second room in the apartment and approached the sleeping form in the bed. Very gently she shook the thin shoulder not covered by the white sheet.

The soft, regular breathing sounds of sleep stopped, replaced by a drowsy sigh. A head covered by floppy brown hair turned, and huge, dark, confused eyes set in a too-lean face fastened on hers. A tide of love swept over her, nearly causing her to take a step backward.

"Hey, Chris," she said, sweeping the hair back from her brother's face. "Sorry to wake you, but we've got to get you packed."

He nodded once, then sat up, the covers falling away to reveal the white T-shirt he wore over his scrawny chest.

"Okay," he said.

Last night, when she'd taken him to the carnival, he'd balked at the roller coaster but had eaten cotton candy and gone on the merry-go-round like any other ten-year-old.

Now his eyes were solemn and he didn't even ask why she was going to upend their lives once again.

Jill wasn't the only one who knew the most effective way to elude a bird dog was to fly off before the hunting party arrived.

CHAPTER ONE

Ten months later

TRUST NO ONE.

Jill Jacobi had managed to follow that simple rule since she'd stumbled across the evocatively named Indigo Springs on a Pennsylvania map and headed there. The scenic Pocono Mountain town had turned out to be a fine place to hide. It was out of the way, yet full of interesting, stimulating people.

No wonder she'd let down her guard.

"It was real sweet of you to invite me over." Jill spoke to Penelope Pollock in a whisper on a Friday night in July. "Even though I haven't known you long, I already love you to death. I might change my mind, though, if you're aiming to fix me up with the vet."

Penelope transferred four bottles of beer from the refrigerator to the sleek granite countertop of the island in her kitchen, then rummaged in a drawer until she pulled out a bottle opener.

"Of course I'm fixing you up." Penelope spoke without a trace of shame. "It's what I do."

Jill would never tell Penelope the truth of how she and Chris had ended up in Indigo Springs. So why hadn't she been more cautious when she'd gotten a dinner invitation from the woman who fancied herself a matchmaker?

The answer was simple, yet complicated.

Jill, who could afford to trust no one, was too darn trusting.

"You should be thanking me." Penelope popped the top on one of the beer bottles. "Dan's a great guy. On the quiet side, but animals and kids love him. When are they ever wrong about a person?"

On the wooden deck visible through the sliding glass doors, Penelope's husband, Johnny, tended the grill as Dan Maguire bent to pet a huge dog. The beast's thick tail wagged vigorously as the dog tried to lick his face. Dan straightened, teeth a dentist would admire flashing as he laughed, his hand still buried in the dog's white-and-mahogany coat.

"I'm sure he's a nice guy," Jill began.

"Nice doesn't begin to cover it," Penelope retorted. "After he started working for Stanley Kownacki, all I heard about him were good things. Now that we have a puppy, I wouldn't dream of using any other vet."

Puppy? That monstrosity of a dog was a *puppy?*

"Not many nice guys are as good-looking as he is," Penelope continued without taking a breath. "Just try to tell me he's not hot."

A breeze rustled Dan's black hair, which fell almost to his collar. Jill knew from the few times she'd happened to see him around town that his eyes were a startling blue, but they weren't his best feature. Neither were his long interesting nose, lean high cheekbones or wide full mouth.

Her eyes dipped to his legs, left bare beneath his khaki shorts. Lean and lightly sprinkled with brown hair, they had excellent calf definition.

Yeah, she was a leg girl, all right.

"Oh, he's hot," Jill said, "but I seem to remember you saying no when I asked if anyone besides you and Johnny would be here."

Wielding the bottle opener in her right hand, Penelope methodically popped the rest of the beer-bottle tops.

"So I lied," Penelope said. "Would you have come if you knew I thought you should get busy with the hot vet?"

"No," Jill replied. "I don't want to get busy with anyone."

"Why is that exactly?" Penelope tossed back her long light brown hair and gazed at Jill out of big dark eyes. "You don't even date."

The response that sprang to mind was that a life on the run with a ten-year-old left no room for romance. Jill swallowed the words for a version of the truth. "Between work and Chris, I don't have time."

"Nonsense," Penelope refuted. "Your landlady treats you and Chris like her grandchildren. You said she doesn't even consider it babysitting to stay home with Chris."

"Then maybe I'm not in the market for a man."

"What kind of talk is that?" Penelope's hand flew to her throat. "The only acceptable reason not to be looking for a man is if you're gay. And in that case, I know a woman I can set you up with."

Jill laughed despite not even being close to getting her point across. There was something endearing about a recent bride wanting everyone else to be as happily in love as she was.

"Not that there's anything wrong with it," Jill said, borrowing a line from one of her favorite sitcoms, "but I'm not gay."

"Then give the vet a whirl, see where things lead. As far as I can tell, Dan doesn't date either, but how can he resist you?" Penelope nodded toward the deck. "See. He's checking you out."

Jill's eyes locked with Dan's through the glass door. She recognized a familiar trapped look and broke the gaze.

"You didn't tell him I'd be here, did you?" Jill accused.

"What difference does that make?" Penelope avoided looking at her. "You have no idea how hard it is to get that man to accept a dinner invitation."

"He probably smelled a setup."

"If you're so against being set up," Penelope said, handing two of the beers to Jill, "why did you just suck in your stomach and stick out your boobs?"

"I did no such thing!" Jill denied before her inherent honesty got the best of her. "Okay, maybe I did suck in my stomach, but I sure didn't do anything with my boobs."

Penelope giggled. "I knew you liked him!"

Jill couldn't help but laugh. "I like everybody," she said. "Even you."

She followed her friend over the kitchen tile, pausing when Dan slid the door open, so she could check where the dog was. The "baby monster," thankfully, was amusing itself in the yard.

The outdoors smelled like freshly mowed grass and grilled hot dogs and hamburgers, yet as Jill handed Dan one of the beers she caught the scent of soap and clean warm skin.

"We come bearing great gifts," Penelope announced, walking straight into her husband's arms. Johnny's grin lit up his entire face, transforming his average looks. He kissed her soundly while the smoke from the grill swirled around them.

"I was referring to the beers," Penelope said when they broke apart, handing her husband one of the cold brews, "but save that thought for later."

Johnny chuckled and went back to tending the food on the grill. "So Penelope tells me you two are dating," he remarked casually as he flipped a burger.

"What?" Jill asked, a question echoed by Dan.

"We don't even know each other." Jill looked fully at Dan. He shuffled his feet, as though he was considering making a run for the hills. "Although I have seen you once or twice at the Blue Haven."

"Of course. You bartend there." It couldn't be more obvious that he'd just put it together why she looked familiar.

"Jill also works at Indigo River Rafters as a guide." Penelope's smile was almost blinding. "I can't wait for you two to get acquainted."

"Penelope." Johnny gestured to his wife with the stainless steel flipper. "You need to stay out of—"

Penelope was close enough to Johnny to plant another kiss on his lips before he could finish the sentence.

Jill edged closer to Dan, shielded her mouth with her hand and whispered, "I truly am sorry. Believe me, I had nothing to do with this."

"I figured that." His answering whisper came through

clenched teeth. In ventriloquist fashion, he barely moved his lips. "It doesn't look like Johnny did, either."

Jill kept her hand in place. "Any ideas on how we can thwart her plans?"

A corner of his mouth quirked. This close to him she could make out the beginnings of his five-o'clock shadow and the thickness of his black eyelashes over those blue, blue eyes. The man really did have dramatic coloring. "We shouldn't make eyes at each other at dinner."

She laughed aloud.

"What's funny?" Penelope asked. She and Johnny were no longer locked at the lips, although Jill wasn't exactly sure when that had happened.

Dan hesitated. "It's a private joke."

Jill widened her eyes and gave him what she hoped was an imperceptible shake of her head. She could tell by his blank look he couldn't decipher her silent message.

"Oooh," Penelope said. "That sounds intimate."

Dan winced. Now he understood.

They ate outside on the deck at a picnic table that overlooked a small backyard bracketed by trees and infused with the lush green that characterized the mountain town in the summer months.

The meal started favorably enough, with Johnny telling an amusing story about a do-it-yourselfer who called his construction company to the rescue after remodeling his own kitchen. The space he'd left for a refrigerator was six feet high—and eighteen inches wide.

"You want construction humor, I've got a true story for you." Dan had a deep, velvety voice that would have been perfect for the radio, making him a pleasure to listen to. "A couple back in Ohio live in a one-room log cabin with a quarter horse. They even set a place for him at the table."

"That sure doesn't sound sanitary." Jill made a face. "I mean, what happens when nature calls?"

"They claim the horse is housebroken. Even lets himself out when he gets the urge."

Everybody laughed, then tried to top each other with increasingly outrageous stories. Before long, Jill let down her guard and started to enjoy herself.

"So, Dan," Penelope said during a rare lull in conversation when they were nearly through with dinner, "I'm sure Jill would love to hear how you became a vet."

Johnny sent his wife a pointed look. "We *all* would."

"Sure you don't want to hear more about the housebroken horse?" Dan took a handful of purple grapes from the bowl on the table and popped a few into his mouth. "He's really quite amazing. When it gets hot, he turns on the ceiling fan."

"You're just as interesting," Penelope said.

"Not by a long shot." Dan rubbed the back of his neck. "Let's see. I grew up in Ohio in a family of Irishmen. Make that Irish*women*. My dad was a salesman who wasn't around much and I've got three older sisters. Even our dog was female."

"And?" Penelope prompted when he stopped talking.

"And we lived near a farm that had a couple boys my age," he continued. "I loved it there. At first just hanging around the boys, then for the animals, and my interest grew."

"Stanley and Dan don't only treat house pets," Penelope announced.

"We're equal opportunity." Dan smiled. It was a nice smile, warm and inviting. "Horses, cattle, sheep. We've got them covered."

"Why did you leave Ohio?" Jill asked.

He hesitated. "It was a good career opportunity."

He took another bite of his burger. He wasn't comfortable talking about himself—that much was clear. He especially didn't want to discuss why he'd moved to Indigo Springs. Jill could relate.

"Does your family still live in Ohio?" Penelope had either failed to pick up on his evasiveness or was having none of it, probably the latter.

"Yes," he said after a pause. "My parents live in the same house where I grew up. My sisters and their families aren't far away."

"You're the only one who isn't married?" Penelope asked.

"That's right."

Dan shifted on the picnic-table bench. Jill fought not to squirm, too. Who knew what Penelope would ask next? The other woman leaned forward, as though about to pounce with a particularly juicy question.

"Dan's true mission on earth leaves him no time for a relationship," Jill announced.

"Excuse me?" Penelope spoke up, but three pairs of eyes regarded Jill curiously.

"Dan seems like an average guy, a simple vet going about his business." Jill lowered her voice. "Except that's only a cover."

"Oh, really?" The corners of Dan's mouth quirked.

"Really." Jill looked over her shoulder, then let her gaze roam over the yard. She returned her attention to her audience, quieting her voice even more. "Did you ever wonder why we don't see much of him in town?"

"I work a lot," Dan said.

"And not just at being a vet. It all stems, of course, from those five world-changing words spoken to you in high school by that stuffy British librarian." She paused for effect, then called upon her most dramatic delivery. "'You are the chosen one.'"

Dan's dark eyebrows lifted.

"This is getting good." Johnny put both elbows on the table and leaned forward. "Chosen for what?"

"To stand alone against the vampires, the demons and the forces of darkness," Jill finished, and drained the rest of her beer, setting the bottle down with a plop.

"Hey, that sounds familiar," Penelope said slowly, then brightened. "I know where I've heard it before. On TV at the beginning of *Buffy the Vampire Slayer* reruns. Buffy's the one girl in all the world who can do that stuff."

"What's to say Buffy doesn't have a male coworker?" Jill asked flippantly. "You've got to admit it explains that tall, dark and enigmatic thing Dan has going on."

"Enigmatic?" A dimple appeared in Dan's left cheek. "No one's ever called me that before."

"That's what you get for not chatting up the bartender at the Blue Haven." She put up a hand so he wouldn't get the wrong idea. "Not that I'm complaining. Most people talk my ear off."

"That's how Jill and I became friends," Penelope

said. "A girlfriend stood me up when Johnny was out of town. I sat at the bar all night talking to Jill. She's an excellent conversationalist. You should ask her to tell you about herself, Dan."

"No need," Dan said as Jill was trying to mentally unearth one of her practiced scripts. "I already know her secret."

Jill heard blood pounding in her ears but forced herself to smile. Dan couldn't possibly know anything about her. He was simply having fun by following her lead.

"Ever wonder why she tones down that Southern accent of hers?" Dan asked. "It's because she doesn't want anyone to know exactly where she's from."

Jill hid her shock that he'd hit the mark even as Penelope said, "Jill's from South Carolina."

"That's what she wants you to believe. The truth is that Jill—" he gestured toward her with his index finger, making his captive audience wait "...is hiding out here in Indigo Springs."

The blood rushed from her head. She clutched at the lip of the picnic table, feeling as though she might pass out. How had Dan figured out her secret? Did he know about Chris, too?

"What's she hiding from?" Penelope asked in an amused, playful voice.

Jill's lungs squeezed, making it impossible to draw in air. She fought not to react under Dan's scrutiny as she waited for his reply.

"Some serious bad guys," he finally answered. "She went to the cops after she witnessed Michael Corleone off two guys in a restaurant. With the mob and the godfather after her, witness protection was the only way to go."

Penelope slapped the table and laughed. "That's almost as good as Danny the Vampire Slayer."

"One preposterous turn deserves another." Looking pleased with himself, Dan finished off his beer.

Oxygen once again reached Jill's lungs, yet the corners of her mouth still felt strained from holding up her fake smile. "Very funny."

Needing a moment longer to compose herself, she rose from the table, gathered her napkin and empty paper plate and dumped them in the trash bag hanging from the corner of the deck.

The tail end of Dan's story had taken a turn for the ridiculous, yet she was shaken at how close he'd come to the truth. Because she and Chris needed to be poised to run, she'd been very careful not to get involved with any man.

It had probably been a fluke, but just in case Dan Maguire was particularly insightful, she had even more reason to avoid him.

NIGHT HAD FALLEN on Indigo Springs, muting the vibrant green of the grass and the clear blue of the sky. The Poconos town came close to Dan's idea of paradise, complete with a crime rate so low it was nearly nonexistent. Yet for some reason he'd insisted on walking Jill Jacobi home.

On one hand, it made sense. She lived only a few blocks from the house his sisters called his hideaway, so they were heading in the same direction. And it wasn't as though he didn't enjoy her company.

If he were ready to date again, he might even ask her out.

"That sure was crazy." Jill peered sideways at him as they walked. She couldn't have been taller than five foot two or three, a marked contrast to Maggie, who was only a couple of inches shy of his six-one. "Did you get a look at Penelope's face when you offered to walk me home? I swear, she's probably planning our wedding as we speak."

"Not a smart move, in retrospect," he said.

"Not smart at all," she agreed cheerfully. "Now that Penelope's hopes are up, she'll be heartbroken if we don't go out on a date."

Whoa. That sounded suspiciously as if she were warming to the idea. Had he given Jill the wrong impression? He'd been confident throughout the night she was no more romantically inclined toward him than vice versa. Now he wasn't so sure.

"I don't know how to say this," he began.

"Whatever it is, just spit it out," she advised. "That's usually the best way."

"Okay." He took a deep breath. "First off, let me say I had a really good time tonight."

They'd reached a residential section of town on a hilly street lined with modest houses, some of which had to be more than one hundred years old. She stopped directly under a street lamp that gave off more light than the crescent moon.

Her short, curly hair framed a face that was compelling rather than beautiful. Her nose turned up at the end, a smattering of freckles dotted her cheeks and nose and her eyes were big for her face. She had a style all her own, with jangling bracelets, oversize jewelry and a funky miniskirt that showed off slim, shapely legs.

"I thought you were going to spit it out," she reminded him.

"I am." He gazed into her eyes. They were either green or gray; he couldn't tell even with the artificial light shining down on them. Hoping he wouldn't hurt her feelings, he said, "I don't want to date you."

She dragged a hand across her forehead and blew out a loud breath. "That's a relief."

Whatever reaction he'd been expecting, it wasn't that one. "It is?"

"Ye-ah." She drew out the word so it sounded as though it had two syllables. "I thought there for a minute you were going to ask me out. I was trying to figure out how to let you down easy."

"Hold on." This did not compute. "You weren't angling for a date when you said that thing about Penelope's heart breaking?"

She let loose with a low-throated laugh, and he didn't know how to feel. "Of course not. Penelope's a sweetheart. But even though she's in love with love, I don't feel responsible for feeding her obsession. Don't get me wrong—you're as cute as can be. But I'm not interested in you."

Cute. He was *cute?*

"Why not?" he heard himself ask.

She stopped laughing, obviously taken aback by the question. And why shouldn't she be? He was, too.

"It's not you," she said slowly. "It's me."

He cringed at her use of the classic breakup cliché when they'd never even been on a date.

"It's not the right time for me to get involved with anybody," she said.

She was in her mid to late twenties, the age many women viewed as the perfect time to settle down. She put up a slim, pretty hand and waved it back and forth, her bracelets softly clanging against each other.

"I have a lot of things going on in my life," she continued. "And let's face it, it's not like you find me attractive."

"I said I didn't want to date you," he corrected quickly. "Not that I wasn't attracted to you."

Her mouth gaped. "You're attracted to me?"

She'd twirled a lock of her curly black hair around her index finger. Bracelets jingled from her arm. The light caught the freckles on her nose, making them look more pronounced.

His mouth went dry.

"You're quite pretty," he said.

Her smile started slowly, then grew wider, revealing even, white teeth.

"Thank you," she said. "But the answer will still be no if you ask me out."

"You're not curious how we'd be together?" he asked. Now, where had that come from?

"Not particularly," she said.

"I thought you said I was…" Oh, Lord, he was actually going to repeat the word. "Cute. Who knows? We might have good chemistry."

She shook her head. "Probably not."

He reached out and touched her hair, which was as soft and springy as it looked. When she didn't back away, he moved his hand to her cheek and gently ran his fingers over her smooth, tanned skin. His eyes drifted to her mouth.

"There's one way to find out."

Her lips parted. He waited for them to form a no, but all that came out of her mouth was warm, sweet-smelling breath.

He slid his palm to the soft skin of her neck and gently cupped the base of her skull. She leaned into his touch, her chin tipping, her lips tilting upward.

Such full, pretty lips.

She was standing slightly uphill from him, which partially made up for their difference in height. He pressed his mouth gently against hers, breathing in her breath, feeling her lips cling to his. It would have been the sweetest of kisses if not for the instant hardening of his body, which he hoped like hell she didn't notice.

No pressure, he told himself as he fought not to deepen the kiss, contenting himself with tracing the seam of her mouth with his tongue. No demands, he thought as he worked his way from one edge of her mouth to the other with a series of soft kisses. Just a simple experiment in sexual chemistry. She'd braced her hand on his heart, which felt as if it might combust.

She pulled back first.

"That was nice," she said, smiling at him pleasantly with her well-kissed lips, "but I still don't want to go out with you."

He blinked a few times, trying to clear the sexual fog clogging his head, attempting to get his body under control.

"I live over there." She indicated a two-story Victorian house that seemed far too large for one person. She headed for it, picking up speed as she went.

"Thanks for walking me home," she called over her shoulder when she reached the top step of a wraparound porch. Baskets of hanging flowers that were probably a riot of color in the daylight hung from the porch in strategic locations.

"You're welcome." His reply was automatic, although a different response rang in his head.

Why the hell didn't she want to date him?

The thud of the door closing jarred him back to his senses. He moved away from the streetlight, into the relative darkness of the sidewalk where he could rationalize away what had just happened.

He'd reacted strongly to Jill because she was the first woman he'd kissed since Maggie had done a number on his heart almost a year ago.

In all that time, he hadn't been tempted to date anyone.

He still wasn't.

So why was he already looking forward to the next time he ran into Jill Jacobi?

CHAPTER TWO

JILL LEANED AGAINST the smooth plane of the closed door, marveling at the show of nonchalance she'd been able to pull off, aware she had only seconds to get her heart to stop pounding and blood to quit racing.

"I'm in the living room, dear," Felicia Feldman called. No surprise there. Jill had seen the fluttering of the curtain covering a front window as she approached the house.

Felicia sat in her favorite armchair in front of the television, the remote control in hand, her gray hair in stark contrast to the floral pattern of the chair. The air smelled of freshly baked bread, one of Felicia's specialties. Jill never took for granted how lucky she and Chris were to live in this house with this wonderful woman.

"Who was that young man you were kissing, dear?" Felicia had already muted the sound of the program she was watching. On the screen, a lineup of nervous young women waited to see whether the hunk in the tuxedo would hand them a rose.

If Dan Maguire were the rose giver and Jill one of the contestants, would she be angling for a flower? Jill pressed together her still-warm lips, preferring not to think about it.

"Hey, Felicia." Jill smiled at her. "*The Bachelor* a rerun tonight?"

"Why, yes." Felicia's lips parted and she nodded. "How did you know that?"

"You wouldn't be looking out the window if it wasn't."

Felicia's laugh had a smoker's raspy quality even though she'd said she quit years ago. "You're right about that. I guess my mind was drifting. I wondered when you'd get home, I opened the curtain and there you were."

"Chris is okay, isn't he?" Jill was relatively sure of the answer. Felicia had her cell phone number in case of emergency.

"Oh, yes, yes. He went to bed a little while ago. Your brother is no trouble at all. Quiet as a mouse, that boy is."

"I appreciate you looking out for him more than you can know."

"Like I told you when you moved in," Felicia said, "I'm glad to do it."

The older woman had also confided she'd decided to rent out rooms after a scare in which she'd nearly lost her home to foreclosure. Her great-nephew, who lived in town, kept trying to help with mortgage payments, but she was having none of that.

Felicia had soon been treating Jill and Chris like family. A widow in her seventies with no children of her own, Felicia embraced the grandmotherly role, looking out for Chris while Jill wasn't home and whipping up fabulous home-cooked meals for all three of them.

"I'll let you get back to your program, then," Jill said, and turned. "I'm calling it a night."

"You can't turn in yet," Felicia protested. "You haven't told me about your evening."

Jill sucked in a breath through her teeth and did a cheerful about-face. She reentered the room and perched on the arm of the sofa, which was covered in the same flowery fabric as the chair.

"I had a very good time," Jill said. "Johnny Pollock grilled burgers the size of your head."

Felicia's hands flew north and traced the shape of her scalp. "Really?"

Jill laughed. "Not exactly, but close. That man cooks a big burger. Penelope made these white-chocolate brownies for dessert that about melted in my mouth. I can get you the recipe if you like."

"Please do." Felicia enjoyed few things in life more than baking, as evidenced by the delicious smells that regularly wafted through the house.

"Penelope was a hoot, as usual. She and Johnny just passed their one-year anniversary. She bought a dozen plastic leis and left them all over the house until Johnny got the hint and booked a trip to Hawaii. They're going next week."

"Hawaii!" Felicia parroted. "How nice!"

The television camera panned to a close-up of a euphoric bachelorette clutching a rose. It cut away to a shot of the woman and the bachelor sharing a kiss in a hot tub, a moment that appeared to have helped the woman's cause.

Jill hadn't stuck around to discover if Dan had been about to hand her the verbal equivalent of a rose after their amazing kiss. She couldn't have accepted if he had, not when the tale he'd spun about her was so close to the truth.

She tore her eyes from the TV and banished Dan from her mind.

"Johnny's remodeling their house. The kitchen's pretty as a picture with stainless steel appliances, mahogany cabinets, granite countertops and this wonderful wood floor. We ate on the back deck, which could be featured in a home and garden magazine." Jill stood up again. "And that's about all there is to tell."

"But you haven't said anything about the man you were kissing!" Felicia caught Jill's hand. "My eyesight isn't what it used to be, but it looked like the vet."

So much for trying to distract the landlady.

"You can see just fine, Felicia." Jill resigned herself to the inevitable. On some level, she'd known she wouldn't get out of the room before she addressed the subject that refused to stay banished. "That was Dan Maguire."

Felicia let go of Jill's hand and clapped hers. "He's so handsome. I hear he's as nice as can be, too. Everybody who takes their pets to him raves about him. Why, he might even be worthy of dating you."

"That's sweet of you to say." Jill bent and kissed Felicia's soft cheek. "But Dan and I aren't gonna be dating."

Felicia's face filled with disappointment. "Why not?"

"Dating is not high on my list of priorities."

Jill's cell phone sounded, the ring tone an upbeat song that spoke of the right to be loved, loved, loved. Penelope's name popped up on the miniature display screen.

"Excuse me," Jill told Felicia. "I need to get this."

"Of course." Felicia's expression telegraphed that she had more to say on the subject. If Jill had learned anything after nearly a year of living with her landlady, however, it was that Felicia was a patient woman. "Good night, dear."

"G'night, Felicia."

The older woman lifted the remote, turning up the sound on the television. Jill headed for the stairs and her second-floor bedroom, but not before a bachelor-ette squealed with excitement over her chance to win the hunk's heart. Jill flipped open the phone. "Hey, Penelope."

"Well?" Penelope demanded, her voice slightly breathless. "What happened?"

"Dan walked me home."

Penelope's sigh came over the phone line loudly and clearly. "I meant what happened *on the walk?*"

Jill's fingers flew to her lips, then trailed across the still-flushed skin of her cheeks.

"Oh, that. Dan and I had a nice long talk about how we didn't want to date each other," she said.

"No! That's not what was supposed to happen. He was supposed to kiss you. It was supposed to be wonderful. You were supposed to develop a thing for each other."

Jill fought off Penelope's romantic scenario.

"I sure am sorry to disappoint you," she said lightly, trying to affect a teasing tone.

"You should be," Penelope declared. "I was positive you two were right for each other."

"Two rights can make a wrong."

There was a beat of silence at the other end of the line. "That's not the saying. Yours doesn't make sense."

"Neither do me and Dan," Jill said as she went into her bedroom and closed the door on her personal sanctuary. She'd painted an accent wall bright yellow and bought a matching bedspread, creating a sunny atmosphere. "So you can stop matchmaking."

"You might as well tell me to quit breathing!" Penelope exclaimed. "Matchmaking is what I do. You know that. But I need a little help to succeed. If Dan isn't your type, who is?"

Jill plopped down on her bed and slipped off her sandals. "I don't have a type."

"Then tell me about the last guy you dated back home in South Carolina."

Jill had to clamp her teeth together to stop from pointing out her home state was Georgia. How she hated lying to her friends—to anyone, really. Her way of dealing was to reveal as little about herself as possible, which meant saying next to nothing about Ray Williams.

"You don't want to hear about him," Jill said. "He couldn't have been more wrong for me."

"I most certainly do want the scoop on your ex!" Penelope declared. "But not tonight. Johnny must not know I'm on the phone. I can hear him calling me from upstairs."

"Then you should go."

"It sounds like he's in the bedroom. So, believe me, I'm going," Penelope said with gusto, then laughed. "We'll talk more later. Early in the week's not good and we're leaving for Hawaii Friday. Can you do lunch either Wednesday or Thursday?"

"I'm working on the river Thursday." Jill's bartending schedule allowed her to guide three or four groups of white water rafters per week, most of the trips concentrated later in the week and on weekends. "On Wednesday I'm having lunch with Chad Armstrong."

"The pharmacist?" Penelope sounded surprised. "*He's* your type?"

"He's a friend." Jill would have been more accurate in reporting Chad was an acquaintance. They'd served together a few months ago on the planning committee for the spring festival. "He needs to talk to me about something."

"Sounds like he's interested in you," Penelope said.

"That's not it." If Chad were romantically inclined toward her, Jill would have picked up on it. "It has to be something else."

"Any idea what?" Penelope asked.

"None," Jill said. "Guess I'll find out Wednesday."

"We'll get together when I get back from Hawaii, then," Penelope said. "I want to hear what your ex did to sour you on other men."

"I'm not sour on men," Jill denied. Her view of human nature was too positive to let one traitorous man she hadn't even loved turn her against the male sex.

"Good," Penelope said. "Then there's hope for you yet."

She rang off, leaving Jill wishing she could be more open with her friend. Penelope could be a touch overbearing, but like Felicia Feldman, she wanted the very best for Jill.

Trust no one.

Jill mentally repeated the mantra that shouldn't have

been so hard for her to follow. She'd already been burned twice, first by Ray, then by the neighbor in whom she'd foolishly confided in Savannah.

No. She couldn't tell Penelope how Ray had tried to sabotage her efforts to get Chris out of Atlanta any more than she could disclose her attraction to Dan.

After that kiss tonight, she couldn't afford to let Penelope finagle another situation where Dan's magnetism might get the better of her common sense.

THE CROWD AT ANGELO'S restaurant seemed particularly thick on Wednesday afternoon as Dan settled into a chair at a table across from Stanley Kownacki.

Maybe it was often this crowded at Angelo's for lunch. In the year that Dan had lived in Indigo Springs he'd eaten there only once, and that was for dinner.

"This is a view of you I don't often see." Stanley leaned back in his chair. He was a big-boned man in his late sixties with a head of dark brown hair that didn't match his graying whiskers.

"We don't eat out together much," Dan pointed out. They wouldn't be having lunch now if Stanley hadn't pushed. Although he seldom acted like it, Stanley was Dan's boss. Today he wouldn't accept the excuse that Dan was too busy to break for lunch.

Stanley's laugh was a pleasant, low rumble. "I meant I don't usually see you sitting down. You work too hard."

"So do you," Dan countered. "What choice do we have? We're booked solid every day."

"That's what I wanted to talk to you about." Stanley gestured to the menu on the table. "Go ahead and decide what to order first. I recommend the fettuccine Alfredo." He put his fingers to his lips and kissed the tips. "Divine."

"I'll have that, too." Dan ignored the menu. He was far more interested in what Stanley had to say than the food.

A skinny waitress with dishwater-blond hair who appeared to be about seventeen approached their table carrying a tray containing four glasses of water. The glasses knocked against each other with each step she took, some of the water sloshing over the brims.

Her eyes cast frantically about, probably for somewhere to set down her burden. Finding no empty surfaces, she slipped one hand under the tray. Dan half rose and took two of the glasses before she could attempt the balancing act.

"Thank you." Her tremulous smile revealed a mouthful of braces. "I'll be back in a minute to take your order."

"We're ready now, sweetheart," Stanley said. "Two fettuccine Alfredos. Extra garlic bread. A root beer for me. How 'bout you, Dan?"

"Coke's fine."

The young waitress glanced down at the order pad sticking out of the pocket of her half apron. The two remaining water glasses bobbled. The pad remained where it was.

"Okay," she said without much conviction, then left.

Dan followed her slow retreat, rooting for her to get where she was going without incident. His gaze slid past the waitress and alighted on a woman with her back to him. Even if a hat had covered her short, curly dark hair, he'd have recognized Jill Jacobi. She had an innate grace and certain way of holding her head that telegraphed she was giving you her full attention.

It seemed she was focused on the man across the table from her. He was about Dan's age, with a familiar face Dan couldn't place.

"See someone you know?" Stanley asked, then laughed. "Of course you do. Half the people in this restaurant bring their pets to us."

"Actually," Dan said slowly, "I see someone I probably should know."

"Who's that?"

"The blond guy in the white dress shirt and blue tie. Glasses. About my age."

Stanley took a look at the table Dan indicated. "That's Chad Armstrong. He's a pharmacist at the drugstore downtown."

Dan hadn't filled a prescription since he'd moved to town, but could picture the man quietly going about his work on the raised counter at the back of the store.

"What else can you tell me about him?" Dan asked.

"You know Sierra Whitmore? The doctor? He dated her for years before she started going with that newspaper reporter. Ben Nash, I think his name was. Moved with him to Pittsburgh, she did."

He'd heard something about the reporter coming to town to solve a decades-old mystery, but he was far more interested in Armstrong. So the pharmacist was single. Were he and Jill on a lunch date? Wasn't Jill supposed to have too much going on in her life to date anyone?

"Why do you ask?" Stanley asked.

"No reason."

Stanley gave him a dubious look.

"I know the woman with him," Dan conceded.

"You mean Jill? The gal who bartends at the Blue Haven?"

"She was at the Pollocks' the other night when they had me over for a barbecue." Dan shifted in his seat. "She's nice."

"That she is," Stanley agreed.

"So what is it you wanted to discuss?" Dan changed the subject before the other vet could say more. "How business is too good?"

"Exactly." Stanley stabbed the air with his finger. "We're too busy. I had to tell a farmer last week we couldn't take on his animals. There isn't enough time in the day."

Jill was directly in Dan's line of vision. She angled her head and laughed at something the pharmacist said. Was the guy really *that* funny? He forced himself to concentrate on the conversation at his table.

"Are you thinking of hiring another vet?" Dan asked.

The present practice had long been a two-man operation, with Dan replacing a vet who had retired a year ago. Stanley and Dan had met at a professional conference, a connection that led to the job offer at a time Dan was badly in need of a scenery change.

"Can't," Stanley said. "Don't have the office space for it and don't want to find a bigger place. I'm thinking of retooling."

Dam stopped trying to figure out the significance of

the way Jill was leaning forward and concentrated on Stanley. "What do you mean retooling?"

"Bob Verducci gave me a call the other day," Stanley said. Verducci had a practice a few miles outside town that also treated both large and small animals. "Fewer people are bringing their pets to him, so he's switching to large animals only."

"Will that have any effect on us?"

"Sure will. You know how the hours build up when you're driving to ranches and stables. If we go small, we can cut way down on the length of our work days."

Dan frowned, although Stanley's reasoning made perfect sense. "I enjoy working with large animals."

"We won't drop that part of our practice entirely," Stanley said. "Bob will handle the bulk of calls for farm animals and horses, but he'll occasionally need backup."

"Why don't we split the work fifty-fifty?"

The young waitress appeared at their table, wisps of hair escaping her ponytail. She set one plate of bruschetta and another of mozzarella sticks on the table. "Your appetizers."

"They look great," Dan said, then added gently, "except we didn't order appetizers."

Her face blanching, she immediately scooped up the plates. "I'm so sorry. I guess you can tell it's my first day."

"It's not a big deal," Dan rushed to reassure her. "You'll get the hang of it in no time."

"You really think so?" Her voice sounded small.

"I do," Dan said. "You already have the tableside manner down."

The waitress was smiling when she left them.

Stanley pointed his index finger at Dan and declared, "That's why a fifty-fifty split won't work."

"Come again?"

"That charm of yours. Why do you think Verducci has been losing business? People want you to take care of their pets. You enjoy that kind of work, too, don't you?"

"I do," Dan confirmed.

"Then there's no problem," Stanley said. "You can take the occasional call when Verducci needs help. The rest of the time, you won't have to work so late."

"I don't mind working late." Just last week Dan had been up half the night helping a cow through a difficult birth.

"All you've done since you got here is work," Stanley said. "Look at it this way. It'll free up your time so you can ask out Jill over there."

"What makes you think I want to do that?"

Stanley's laugh rumbled forth. "Besides the way you're staring at her?"

"She's pretty," Dan said lamely.

"So go for it," Stanley said. "Stop working so hard and have some fun."

The young waitress made another pass by their table, presenting Dan with a calzone and setting an individual pepperoni pizza in front of Stanley.

"Wrong again, sweetheart," Stanley said. "We both ordered fettuccine Alfredo."

Her lower lip quivered and she appeared to fight tears as she picked up the plates. "These must belong to that couple over there. Forgive me. Please."

"Don't give it another thought," Dan said, but she was already moving away.

Nothing but linoleum floor stretched between the waitress and the table where Jill dined with the pharmacist. There was absolutely no reason the girl should stumble, but she did. The calzone, the pizza and the plates went momentarily airborne, then clattered to the floor.

Dan leaped up from his chair, reaching the scene of the calamity in seconds. Jill was already there, her hand supporting the young girl's elbow. "Are you all right?"

"I'm fine," the waitress wailed, "but the food's ruined!"

"Don't you worry about that." Jill patted her arm soothingly. Today she was dressed in another eye-catching outfit: pink, turquoise and white madras shorts that skimmed her knees, a lacy turquoise camisole blouse and dangling earrings. "Everyone makes mistakes when they start out waitressing. If they say they don't, they're lying."

"Really?"

"Really," Jill said.

Dan bent, retrieved the tray, an overturned plate and the calzone. Jill crouched beside him, picking up the other plate and the pizza, which had miraculously landed tomato-sauce side up.

"If it isn't my matchmaker's choice." Jill's smile was impish, the light reaching eyes he now realized were green.

"But not yours," he said.

"Ditto." She kept smiling at him, appearing genuinely

glad to run into him. If he'd learned one thing about her in their short acquaintance, though, it was that she was unfailingly friendly. "Where did you come from?"

He gestured behind them. "I'm having lunch with my boss. I would have waved, but your back was to me."

"Likely story." She winked at him. "Oops. Shouldn't have done that. Don't worry. I stand by what I said the other night. You're safe from my attentions."

Yet she obviously welcomed the pharmacist's interest.

"Thanks so much for helping me pick this up," the waitress said to them both, taking the tray from Dan. "You two are the best."

"Hang in there." Jill got to her feet and Dan followed suit. "Once you get over the opening-day jitters, you'll make a fabulous waitress."

The girl beamed at her. Dan found himself smiling at Jill, too, and curiously reluctant to part from her once the waitress headed back to the kitchen.

"One more thing before I go." Jill's eyes opened so wide that white was visible all around the green irises. "Beware the matchmaker. We've got some breathing room because she's leaving for Hawaii soon, but she's not convinced we aren't perfect for each other. She might try another ambush."

She grinned and turned back to her table before Dan could say anything. That was probably a good thing, because he should keep the response that came to mind to himself until he figured out what to do about it.

Because if Penelope made another stab at setting him up with Jill, he'd be all for it.

"SO WHAT DID YOU WANT to talk to me about?" Jill kept her attention fixed on Chad, fighting the temptation to turn around and sneak another look at Dan.

So far, Jill had done most of the talking. She didn't mind. Chad was a quiet sort. If she didn't press him on the reason he'd asked her to lunch, however, the bill might arrive before he got around to discussing the subject.

He adjusted his wire-rimmed glasses. Was he stalling for time? Could Penelope have been right? Was Chad screwing up his courage to tell her he was interested, that he viewed their lunch as a first date?

She breathed in sharply as she belatedly realized Dan could have sized up the lunch that way. It explained his comment about being her matchmaker's choice but not hers.

She'd informed Dan after the barbecue that it wasn't the right time for her to get involved with anyone. Yet less than a week later she was on what could appear to be a date.

She didn't owe Dan an explanation, yet suddenly she had an overwhelming desire to rush to his table and clarify that she and Chad were just friends.

"Mountain bikes," Chad said.

His answer didn't compute. "Come again?"

"I want to talk about mountain bikes."

"Do you ride?" She hit the trails three of four times a week, but had never bumped into him.

"My friend does." His voice softened, hinting at his feelings for the *friend*. "We went to pharmacy school together. I ran into her at a reunion last weekend and she told me about the ride she's helping to organize across the Poconos."

"I heard about that." Jill no longer belonged to any bike organizations, as she had when she'd managed the shop in Atlanta, but she still checked Web sites for news. "Aren't they calling it the Poconos Challenge?"

"Yes." Chad nodded. "Towns are invited to turn in proposals to host stops along the way. You could make that happen for Indigo Springs."

"Me?" Jill gestured to herself. "I'm afraid I don't understand."

"You ride and you enjoyed working on the spring festival. You're a logical choice to help put together a bid."

She couldn't dispute either of those facts. Neither could she explain why having her old life intersect with her new one would be risky. She hadn't managed to elude the private eye on her tail up to this point by luck alone. She was smart enough not to fall into her old habits.

"It seems to me this is something the mayor's office should act on," Jill remarked.

"Definitely," Chad said. "I just thought you'd put yourself in an advantageous position if you proposed the idea."

"An advantageous position for what?"

"Borough council."

She started. "What makes you think I want to run for the council?"

"When we worked on the festival, you were the one who went to the mayor with ideas about how to improve downtown parking and attract more tourists," he said. "You'd be a natural."

She couldn't refute him. The idea of community politics held surprising appeal. She'd discovered during her civic volunteer work that she had a knack for seeing the big picture, a quality that would serve a council member well.

"Well?" Chad asked. The word was a temptation.

If she spearheaded an effort to bring the bike race to Indigo Springs in conjunction with the community work she'd already done, she'd be in a great position to run for council.

She let herself envision it for a moment. Her name on the ballot. The opportunity to do some good for the fine people of Indigo Springs. The questions the local newspaper would ask in order to print her bio in a special election section.

Who was she kidding? She could no more run for community politics than compete in a Miss Universe pageant.

"Thanks for thinking of me." She was surprised it was hard to smile. "But I'm not going to run for office. You can let the mayor's office know about the bike race yourself."

"Okay. If that's what you want," he said, then grew quiet at the arrival of the rookie waitress and the second coming of their order.

A few moments later Chad reached for a piece of his individually sized pizza, biting into a slice as though nothing notable had happened.

It had, though.

Jill had gotten another reminder that she'd surrendered

her chance to lead a normal life by going on the run with her brother.

She felt a prickly sensation on the back of her neck and turned, her gaze locking with Dan's.

A thrill traveled through her, which was starting to be par for the course. She'd experienced it when they talked over the broken plates and had felt it more strongly during their kiss.

The sensation provided enough incentive for her to break the connection. The reasons she couldn't get involved with Dan hadn't changed, providing ample cause for her to keep her mouth shut about why she was lunching with Chad.

Dan would eventually discover she and the pharmacist weren't an item. She'd be smart to use the time until he did to devise a way to stop the thrill.

CHAPTER THREE

DAN WAVED OFF THE GNATS swirling around his face. He took his time as he hoisted his sturdy mountain bike from the bed of his Jeep to the packed earth of the parking area.

The morning sun highlighted a streak of dust on the handlebars he must have missed when he wiped down the bike. He'd regularly hit the trails back in Ohio. Here in Indigo Springs he'd waited so long to take his inaugural ride he'd had to dig the bike out from a pile of stuff in his garage.

Funny how life worked. If Penelope Pollock hadn't mentioned mountain biking when he ran into her before she left for her second honeymoon, he might not have gotten the notion to take up riding again.

It had all started when Dan made an offhand remark about seeing Jill lunching with Chad Armstrong. Penelope emphatically maintained the two were not dating, a piece of information that fit. Somebody as honest and upfront as Jill wouldn't have fed him a line about her resolve not to get involved with anyone.

Penelope was sketchy on the details but did know the lunch had somehow involved cycling. Chad didn't ride, but Jill did. In fact, on Sunday mornings when she wasn't on the water Jill biked the very trail Dan was about to take.

Dan had parked his Jeep in a small lot near the entrance to the trail, which happened to be among the most popular in the region. A sensible choice for a cyclist aiming to get back into the sport.

He swatted at the pesky gnats again, which only seemed to make more of them appear. The sun beat down, getting warmer by the minute. A bead of sweat trickled down his face.

He really should get moving.

When he didn't budge, he finally had to admit to himself he'd been hoping Jill's ride would coincide with his. Although, come to think of it, the woman was a bartender. His chances of being in the same place at the same time she was would have been infinitely better at the Blue Haven.

Brother, was he out of practice when it came to male-female relations.

He blew out a breath, then sucked in a bigger one, along with what must have been a half dozen gnats. He coughed, trying to clear his throat. He doubled over to spit out the insects, peripherally aware of a soft crunching noise.

He straightened in time to see the back of a mountain bike entering the trail. Jill's black curly hair stuck out from under her bike helmet, while her strong, lithe legs pumped at the pedals.

"Damn," Dan said aloud.

The trail entrance was a few miles from the town center, most of the route uphill, all of it on a narrow, twisting road. It hadn't occurred to him to bike to the trail entrance.

He swung one leg over the crossbar before remembering bike safety and disembarking. Snatching his helmet from the bed of the pickup, he shoved it on his head. Jill had been traveling at a pretty good clip. With her head start, it was possible he wouldn't catch up to her.

The trail appeared to follow a wide loop to the right before bending back around. To his left was a forest consisting mostly of tall oaks interspersed with evergreens.

He took off for the forest, steering his bike between an uneven row of spindly tree trunks. The bike's thick tires flattened the underbrush. Branches and twigs slapped at him. He shielded his face with one hand, navigating the shortcut with relative ease.

The path soon came into view, and he gave himself a mental high five. The going was bumpy, but he and the bike had held up beautifully. They were both made of sturdy stuff, able to withstand a rugged ride.

The thick, low-lying branch came out of nowhere. Dan jerked the handlebars to the left. The wheels stopped spinning, propelling his body weight forward. He squeezed the hand brakes, desperately trying to keep his balance as the bike skidded through the leaves and the dirt.

Then, just shy of the path, it came to a jarring stop.

His heart hammered faster than the beak of a woodpecker against a tree. It seemed incredible that he was upright and in one piece. The bike, though, had taken a hit. Lodged in the spokes of the back wheel was a stick of wood. The chain had come loose.

Sighing, he got off and dislodged the stick. To better assess the damage, he needed to move the bike out of the brush. Before he reached the trail, Jill Jacobi came into view, dressed in black mountain bike shorts, a purple sleeveless shirt and a black helmet decorated with red lightning bolts. She slowed, then stopped, planting her feet on either side of her bike.

"Dan!" she exclaimed. "What are you doing over there?"

Not exactly the scenario he'd envisioned when he'd taken off through the woods to catch up to her.

He slowly wheeled his bike onto the path. "I was about to put the chain back on."

"But how did you…" Her voice trailed off and she tilted her head. Her pretty face scrunched up. "Did you just ride through the woods?"

"Isn't that what we're both doing?"

"I'm on a path," she pointed out.

"I, um, took a shortcut."

"Why?"

Great question.

"It seemed like a good idea at the time," he said.

Her gaze dropped to the dislodged chain. "Not your best move. You haven't done much mountain biking, have you?"

"Can't imagine why you'd think that," he deadpanned. Her laugh was a pleasant rumble. "Believe it or not, I used to ride all the time in Ohio. Looks like we have something in common."

"Don't tell Penelope," she said in a teasing voice.

"Actually, I ran into her a few days ago and your name came up," he said.

"Did you mention me or did she?"

"I did," he admitted. "I said I'd run into you at lunch

with the pharmacist and she assured me you weren't dating."

"That explains why she was trying to reach me before she and Johnny left on their trip." She didn't contradict her friend about Chad Armstrong. "Her message said it was a matter of my dating life or death. I'm telling you, you have to watch what you say around her."

"We could give in and become friends."

That was what he wanted. A friendship that could slowly build into something deeper and richer. Maggie had hurt him badly by keeping secrets behind his back. Jill was the perfect counterpart: open, honest, uncomplicated.

He was finally ready to move on.

"Penelope would never accept there was only friendship between us. No. Better to play it safe." She kept smiling at him, her cheerful expression at odds with her firm rejection. She nodded to his bicycle. "You need any help with that?"

He hadn't required assistance in putting on a bicycle chain in probably twenty years. "If I said yes, you might figure out it was a ploy to keep you around."

"If I didn't know better," she countered, "I'd think you were flirting with me."

"You don't know me as well as you think you do."

She stayed perfectly still, her expression frozen somewhere between shock and an emotion he couldn't identify. A squirrel scampered up a nearby tree, chattering as it went. A bird chirped. The gnats found him again. None of those things could pull his attention from Jill.

A sliver of sunlight was shining on her through a break in the trees, but her light seemed to come from within. Why hadn't he realized until this moment how truly lovely she was?

The moment lengthened until he thought he could hear her breathing. Or maybe those shallow breaths were his own.

"I should get going," she said, shattering the silence.

She balanced one foot on the ground and stepped on a pedal with the other, propelling the bike forward. She shot past him faster than a competitor in the Tour de France.

Now that he'd decided to change her mind about dating him, he needed to figure out how to get her to give him a chance.

Unfortunately that didn't look as if it would happen any time soon.

"JILL! JILL! WHERE ARE YOU?" Chris barreled into a kitchen that smelled of the pot roast and mashed potatoes Felicia had served for dinner that evening.

He skidded to a stop beside the table, interrupting Jill's latest stab at convincing Felicia Feldman she had no intention of seeing Dan Maguire again, kiss or no kiss.

Both Jill and Felicia set down their coffee mugs.

"Come quick!" Her brother's thin chest heaved up and down. His breathing was ragged, his face red.

"Tell me what's wrong, Chris." Jill's heartbeat accelerated, her mind conjuring up all sorts of reasons for his behavior.

Foremost among them was the fear that the private eye had found them.

"Just come." He grabbed her hand and gave a tug that was surprisingly effective given he was only three or four inches over four feet tall and weighed about sixty pounds. He headed for the back door, practically dragging her with him.

Felicia followed, the landlady's complexion almost as gray as her hair.

"Are you okay, Chris?" Felicia's voice trailed them down the back porch's wooden steps and past the row of azaleas to the patch of woods behind the house. Dusk had fallen, muting the colors of the flowers and lending the early evening a murky quality.

"I'm okay," Chris answered, then said in a voice only loud enough for Jill to hear. "He's not."

"Who's not okay?" Jill demanded.

"You wouldn't believe me if I told you," Chris muttered, then broke into a run before Jill could refute him. Not that she didn't realize Chris had a habit of stretching the truth. She just didn't believe he lied about important things.

His desperation told her this was something important.

Imagining someone in distress, Jill kept up with him even as the muscles in her legs protested. She felt every inch of the twenty-mile mountain-bike trek she'd taken that morning, but she kept going. At least she'd had the presence of mind to grab her cell phone. She could dial 911.

Chris took a shortcut through some tall pines to reach one of the walking trails a local hiking group maintained. She allowed Chris to venture into the woods as long as it was light out and he stayed close to home.

The past few nights he'd been eager to go outside after dinner, hoping to catch a glimpse of the family of deer that sometimes appeared at dusk. He'd vowed to find out where they lived.

Had he stumbled across something while following the deer?

"There!" He broke into a run down the narrow trail, his thin arms and legs moving faster than she'd ever seen them.

Jill squinted, and her breath clogged her throat. Something small that she couldn't quite make out was lying just off the path. Oh please, she prayed, don't let it be a child.

She increased her pace, getting a clearer view as she came nearer. No. It definitely wasn't human. Chris crouched next to an animal of some sort. Light caramel in color, it had four legs, yet its body was too thick to be a fawn.

Was it a stray dog? She immediately thought rabies and had opened her mouth to shout a warning when she heard a...bleat?

The sound came again. Yes, it was definitely a bleat.

"Why, that's not a dog." Jill reached her brother's side and examined the animal's long droopy ears and short, wide face. "It's a goat."

"A baby goat." Chris smoothed his hand over the animal's coat in a rhythmic, calming motion. "That's why I said you wouldn't believe me. Something's wrong with him."

The goat was injured, not sick. Blood matted its coat and it held one of its legs stiffly. She heard the faint roar of a motorcycle engine, a reminder that this section of woods adjoined the two-lane thoroughfare leading to and from downtown Indigo Springs.

"The poor thing. It looks like he might've been hit by a car." The goat could have limped into the woods before it collapsed. But where had it come from? Farms dotted the countryside, but she didn't know of one nearby. "I think his back leg is broken."

"We need to take him to a vet!" Chris cried.

Although the goat measured about two and a half feet from head to hooves, it had a thick, muscular body and probably weighed thirty pounds.

"He's too big to carry," she said.

The animal made a soft, keening sound that tore at Jill.

"Somebody has to help him!" Chris sounded close to tears, stabbing at Jill's heart. On the other hand, she wasn't surprised. Her brother cried while watching lions attack their prey on the National Geographic channel.

Jill placed her hand on her brother's back, feeling his body trembling. "I didn't say we wouldn't help him, honey. Only that we can't move him."

"Then what are we going to do?" Chris wailed.

Jill quickly ran over options in her mind. She could phone a veterinarian, except nightfall was quickly approaching and she didn't know how late vets worked or whether they took after-hour calls.

Or she could fetch one.

"I know of someone who can help." She handed her brother her cell phone. "Stay here and I'll be back as quick as I can."

She took off at a trot, hardly noticing the leaves and

small twigs that slapped at her arms and legs. She did, however, recognize the irony in the situation.

She was running toward the one man from whom she should stay far away.

DAN'S FIRST INDICATION that this wouldn't be an ordinary Tuesday night came when the dogs who'd settled in to watch him fix the kitchen cabinet leaped to their feet and broke into loud barking.

Starsky and Hutch raced for the door, their paws sliding over the hardwood floor.

Dan rose slowly, reluctant to abandon the job he'd finally gotten around to tackling. Almost a year after he'd moved into the small, two-bedroom house, the cabinet was still coming off its hinges.

"Starsky! Hutch! Quiet!" he commanded.

The two mixed-breed dogs kept barking, completely in disregard of the fact that he was a vet with a reputation to uphold.

"You're going to give me a bad name," Dan told the dogs as he nudged past them to the door. Their tails wagged in double time while they panted with undisguised anticipation. "It's also uncool to give the impression that nobody ever visits us."

Starsky barked, almost as if to say they hardly ever did get visitors.

"Point taken, smart aleck," Dan muttered, then swung open the door to a surprise.

"I'm sorry to stop by like this," Jill said in a rush, "but I need you."

The last three words could have been straight out of his fantasies if the delivery had been different. She was out of breath. A slight sheen of perspiration dampened her brow and her curly hair was disheveled.

"What's wrong?" he asked.

"There's a goat in the woods. I think its leg is broken."

"A goat?" The dogs were barking enthusiastically. Dan positioned his body so they couldn't get out of the house and lick her to death.

"The poor thing could really use your help." Her expression was pleading, as though she feared he might say no. Even if he were capable of turning away from an animal, no way could he refuse Jill.

"Sure." He regained his equilibrium, his mind racing as he thought about what he needed to do. "Just give me a minute to gather some supplies. You can wait inside."

The dogs erupted into a cacophony of even louder barks before he could move aside to allow her entrance. She stepped backward.

"They're harmless, I promise you." He grimaced, feeling a telltale flush of embarrassment start up his neck. "They're just overly friendly."

"It'll be easier if I wait for you out here," she said.

He swallowed the urge to tell her the only pets he had trouble getting to behave were his own. There was no time for that. He closed the door, careful to prevent the canines from escaping, then transferred supplies to his backpack from the bag he used for house calls. He added some PVC pipe and a high-powered flashlight and he was ready to go.

They reached the goat in minutes, with Jill setting a breakneck pace. Her haste was more in keeping with someone worried about an injured pet rather than a stray farm animal.

The reason soon became apparent.

The goat wasn't alone.

A young boy of about nine or ten with wavy brown hair was cradling the animal's head in his lap. He gazed up at Dan out of big eyes shaped like Jill's.

Stanley was right, Dan thought. He really had been working too hard if he'd lived in Indigo Springs for nearly a year without realizing this boy existed.

Although with tourists swelling the population, the town wasn't as small as it appeared. Up until a few weeks ago, Jill herself had barely been on Dan's radar screen.

"Please help him," the boy pleaded.

Was he Jill's son? If so, she'd given birth as a teenager. Where, then, was the boy's father? Was the father the reason Jill wasn't in the market for a relationship?

"That's why I'm here. By the way, it's a her, not a him." With the goat lying on its side, Dan could clearly define the sex. "She's not a farm animal, either. She's a pygmy goat."

"You mean she's not a baby?" Chris asked.

"I'd say she's about a year old, so she won't get a whole lot bigger than she already is," he said. "My name's Dan, by the way."

"I'm sorry," Jill cut in. She was standing a shoulder's length from him, yet he was acutely aware of her every movement. "Dan, this is Chris, my brother."

Her brother. Ah, that made more sense. The boy was probably visiting her.

The animal emitted a low noise that sounded almost

like a moan. Dan focused on the goat, his need to alleviate the animal's pain overriding everything else.

"Did either of you see what happened?" He did a visual exam, noting the matted blood on the goat's coat. The scrape on its body, though, was superficial. More worrisome was the way the goat was holding her leg, which indicated a simple fracture.

"I found her right here," the boy said. "Jill thinks she got hit by a car."

"That's a good guess," Dan said. "Lots of people keep pygmies as pets. Either she got loose or someone dumped her on the side of the road."

"No!" Chris cried.

Dan was about to point out dogs and cats were abandoned every day, but the boy needed reassurance more than enlightenment. He could also use a job to help him feel useful.

"I'm pretty sure her leg is broken, but she'll be okay if we all work together," Dan said. "Chris, can you follow directions?"

The boy appeared wary.

"You can be my assistant." He turned the flashlight on and handed it to Chris. "Shine the light on us. This is very important. Be careful not to shine it in the goat's eyes. Can you do that, Chris?"

"I'll try." He sounded unsure of himself, but stood up and did exactly as Dan instructed.

"That's perfect. I'm going to give her a mild sedative and then put some antiseptic on this scrape." Dan worked as he talked. When the goat was breathing more easily and he'd cleaned the abrasion, he looked at Jill.

"I need your help, too, Jill. Place a little pressure on her neck with your elbow. That'll keep her still."

Jill's face might have paled, but she nodded and lowered herself next to the goat. The animal bleated. She jerked backward, took a shaky breath, then in one quick movement placed her elbow in exactly the right spot. Her eyes were closed.

"Good." He hid a smile. "After I wipe down the leg, I'll get the bone back in alignment and put on a temporary splint until I can get her in the office. She won't like this part, so keep the pressure steady."

"Okay." Jill's voice cracked.

He took firm hold of the animal's injured leg, digging his fingers into its flesh so he could gauge the severity of the break. A simple fracture, just as he'd expected.

He pulled on the leg as slowly and gently as he could, manipulating the bone until he had it in alignment.

"This next part's going to be tricky. Chris, see my bag there. I need you to get me a roll of cotton. I'm going to use it for padding. Can you do that?"

Chris didn't answer. A few seconds later, however, he handed Dan the cotton, then got back into position with the flashlight.

Working quickly, Dan wrapped cotton from the top of the goat's hoof to about a half dozen inches above the break.

"Now I need that blue stretchy tape to hold the padding in place," Dan said. Chris rummaged in the bag, came up with the tape, but dropped the flashlight in the process.

"I'm sorry! I'm sorry!" Chris bent and grabbed

for the flashlight, then dropped it again. He sounded miserable.

"Relax, Chris." Dan gentled his voice. "It's not a big deal."

"You're doing fine," Jill added in the same soothing tone.

Dan couldn't take the time to puzzle over the boy's reaction. When the light was back in place, he started the wrap, working as efficiently as he could. Despite the sedative, the goat twitched and keened. Without being told, Jill increased the pressure on the animal's neck. Jill's face was in shadows, but he thought her eyes might still be closed.

"Easy, girl," he said.

Jill's head rose. "She's doing good."

"I was talking to you." He winked at Jill, just in case she could see him.

The rest of the job was easier. The final step involved creating a temporary splint, which he did by securing two halves of PVC pipe with duct tape. The goat tried to stand up as soon as Dan instructed Jill to stop applying pressure. Dan helped it to its feet. It was able to put weight on all four legs but wobbled, still feeling the effects of the sedative.

"How are we going to get her out of the woods?" Jill asked. "She looks pretty shaky."

"I'll carry her." Dan talked while he was gathering his supplies. "Pygmy goats are good-natured, so it shouldn't be a problem."

Dan scooped up the goat, careful not to jostle its injured leg. It squirmed so much he nearly dropped it, then butted his shoulder with its nose and bleated.

"I thought they were good-natured," Jill said.

"They are." He withstood another nose butt. "She associates me with pain."

"I think she likes me," Chris said in a hesitant voice. It was the first remark he'd made since dropping the flashlight.

Jill ruffled the boy's hair. "Of course she does. You found her. You're her hero."

Darkness was quickly approaching, making it necessary for Chris to keep shining the flashlight, this time to illuminate their path. Dan walked as fast as he dared with approximately thirty pounds of goat in his arms.

He almost cheered when they reached the clearing and he could put down the goat, at least temporarily. Chris knelt beside the animal, murmuring soothingly to it.

"You've got a way with that goat, Chris," Dan remarked. "You got any pets?"

Now that they were out of the woods, the crescent moon gave off enough light for Dan to see Chris shake his head. "No."

"Well, you're a natural with her, although I don't imagine you see many goats back home in South Carolina."

Chris didn't look up from where he was petting the goat. "I'm from Georgia."

Dan turned questioningly to Jill. He was certain Penelope had said she was from South Carolina.

"Chris still thinks of Georgia as his home state because he was born there," Jill said, "but he only lived there a few years."

"Where do you live in South Carolina, Chris?" Dan asked.

"Chris lives here." Jill answered for her brother. "With me."

So Chris wasn't visiting, as Dan had originally thought.

"And with Felicia," Jill added.

"Who's Felicia?"

"Our landlady," Jill said, which cleared up the mystery of why she lived in such a large house. "Felicia's a sweetheart, but I'm not sure how she'll react when we show up at the house with a goat."

"My backyard's fenced and I have a shed I can empty out. The goat can stay there tonight," Dan offered.

Jill's response was immediate. "I couldn't ask you to do that."

"Why not?" He smiled at her. She was wearing shorts and tennis shoes, but had given the generic outfit some personality with a tie-dyed T-shirt. "That splint's temporary. I need to get her into the office in the morning anyway so I can put on a cast."

"Are you sure?"

"Absolutely sure." He repositioned the backpack on his shoulder and reached for the goat. "I'll take her, Chris."

Chris held tight to the goat, saying nothing. He didn't need to. He'd clearly developed an attachment he wasn't ready to break.

"Why don't you help me get her settled?" Dan asked.

"I don't think—" Jill began.

"Please can I go, Jill?" Chris interrupted, stark longing on his face. "Please."

"I'd love to have you join us, Jill," Dan was quick to add. "You're not working at the bar tonight, right?"

"I have Tuesday nights off," she confirmed. Her chest rose and fell. Her answer was slow in coming. "Okay."

"Then let's get this goat show on the road," Dan said, and lifted the animal. He hadn't taken more than two steps when the goat's nose butted him one more time.

Considering that the out-of-sorts pygmy goat was providing an in with Jill, he wasn't about to complain.

CHAPTER FOUR

JILL DISCONNECTED the call she'd made to update Felicia on the night's events, then hung back, closer to Dan's house than his backyard shed. The porch light combined with the glow from the moon gave her a clear view of Dan hunkered down beside her much smaller brother.

"Here, Chris. Give Tinkerbell this." Dan handed something orange to her brother. "Goats consider carrots a treat."

"Yuck! I'd want an ice cream cone."

A laugh erupted from Dan.

"I wouldn't eat hay and oats, either." Dan's voice held a chuckle. "But that's what Tinkerbell likes."

Chris had named the goat after the tiny fairy in his favorite book, gaining approval from Dan. Her brother offered the goat the carrot. She sniffed at it, then took it and nibbled.

"You sure she'll be okay out here?" Chris sounded dubious.

"I'm keeping my dogs in the house as a precaution," Dan said, obviously referring to the two champion barkers Jill had seen earlier tonight. "The fence is high enough that nothing can get in or out, but I'll lock the shed tonight just in case."

The three of them had already created space inside

the shed by transferring a lawn mower and assorted tools to the garage.

"What if Tinkerbell's afraid of the dark?" her brother asked.

As Chris was, Jill thought.

"Tinkerbell?" Dan shook his head. "Nah. She stares into the face of darkness and knows there's nothing out there scarier than she is."

Chris giggled. "She's a pygmy goat!"

"She doesn't like to be underestimated because of her size," Dan said.

Chris's giggle became a full-fledged laugh, a noise Jill didn't hear often and hadn't expected to tonight. Her brother was slow in warming up to strangers and typically said little to anyone except her.

She backed away, sinking onto a bench situated under an oak tree, wishing she hadn't learned Dan was as good with kids as he was with animals.

She'd rather have avoided coming to Dan's house altogether, but she couldn't trust Chris alone with him after her brother had slipped up and said they were from Georgia.

Dan straightened, patted Chris on the back and walked toward her, his gait leisurely and self-assured. He wore jeans, but she could see the play of muscles in his long, leanly muscular legs as he moved. She dragged her gaze upward, over his trim waist and broad shoulders to the compelling features of his face. Darn it. There was nowhere safe to look.

"How's it going over there?" Jill kept her expression neutral so he wouldn't catch on that she'd been ogling him.

He sat down next to her, close enough that she could smell the warm, pleasant scent of his skin. "I might have an idea about why Tinkerbell was dumped. I'm pretty sure she's blind in one eye."

"Surely someone wouldn't abandon her for that!" Jill cried.

"People have discarded pets for less," Dan said. "Not people like your brother, though. He won't leave her side."

"Oh, gosh. We're keeping you from something, aren't we?" She half rose. "I'll just go tell Chris we need to leave."

"Hold on." He put a hand on her arm, the first time he'd touched her since their kiss. Her nerve endings came alive, awareness spreading under his fingers. "That wasn't a hint for you to go. I'm enjoying the company. Your brother's a great kid."

"I agree with you there." Jill sat back down, not sure whether she felt bereft or relieved when his hand dropped away. She silently admitted she wasn't ready to leave yet, either. She just thought she should be.

"How old is Chris?" Dan asked.

"Ten. He looks younger because he's small for his age."

"As the shortest boy in his sixth-grade class, I know all about that," Dan said.

"You're kidding me. You must be six-four or six-five."

Dan's laugh was smooth and rich, as deep and attractive as his voice. "I guess I must seem that tall to you, but I'm only six-one."

"Only?" she said.

His laugh got even deeper. "I guess height's relative. Everybody was taller than me when I was Chris's age, even the girls. I didn't get my last four or five inches until I was in college."

"I never would have guessed that," Jill said. "It just goes to show you can't jump to conclusions about people."

"Then maybe you won't mind me asking why he's living with you?"

She did mind, although it would cause him to wonder why if she said so. "My parents divorced when I was eight. Chris and I have the same father, but different mothers. His mama died three years ago of breast cancer."

"That's rough," Dan said. "How about your dad? Is he still alive?"

This was the toughest part of the story for Jill to pull off. Her stomach cramped, as it always did before she lied. "No."

She waved a hand and delivered the second part of the carefully crafted reply before he had a chance to respond.

"I'm sorry. It's hard to talk about." That, at least, was the truth. "I'd appreciate it if you didn't mention his father to Chris. Either of his parents, really."

"Sure." Dan's voice was compassionate, making her feel even guiltier, although circumstances had forced her into the lie. "You can count on me. And if you ever want to talk about it, I'm a good listener."

He was also the right kind of man. Not only did she admire his character, she liked him. If her situation were different, she'd seek out his company.

"What's a nice guy like you doing living here in Indigo Springs all by yourself?" She blurted out the question uppermost in her mind.

He cocked his head, his eyes crinkling at the corners. "Do you mean why am I single?"

"Never mind." She tried to backtrack. "It's none of my business."

"I moved to Indigo Springs after my fiancée left me," he said, staring at the hands in his lap instead of her. "We'd been dating for almost two years, living together for about half that time. One day I came home from work and all her things were gone."

Jill tried to summon the willpower to dissuade him from confiding in her further and failed. There was too much about him she still wanted to know. "Didn't you see it coming?"

"Nope." His tone was self-deprecating. "She's an interior designer. She'd talked about how cool it would be to work in New York City. I could never see myself living in a big city and told her so. I thought that was the end of it."

"But it wasn't?"

"Not for her. She lives in Manhattan with her new husband. He's an actor who does off-Broadway plays. They got married six months ago."

"I sure am sorry," Jill said.

"I'm not." He shrugged, his half smile not reaching his eyes. "Well, not anymore. It hit me pretty hard at first. It's probably even the reason I accepted the job in Indigo Springs. I can finally see it was for the best."

"How so?"

"I found out she'd been planning to leave me for a month, yet she never let on. If she could keep that big of a secret from me, she wasn't the person I thought she was."

Jill understood exactly what he meant. For a relationship to work, the two people involved needed to be open and honest with each other. The way she'd tried to be with her boyfriend in Atlanta before he'd used her confidences to betray her.

The way she'd learned she could never be with anyone as long as she was on the run with her brother.

"I'm making you uncomfortable," Dan said. "Sorry."

"Not at all." Another lie.

"I'm not sure why I told you all that." He let out a breath and shook his head. "Maybe so you'd understand why I thought I wasn't ready to date anyone."

Yet he was now.

It didn't matter that he hadn't said so. Jill heard him loud and clear. Something had changed in the week and a half since the cookout, something that made him amenable to the idea of dating again.

Of dating her.

"Chris and I really should be going." She scrambled to her feet so fast the blood rushed to her head. She fought the light-headedness and moved toward her brother, who was still crouched beside the goat. "Chris! Time to go."

"Just a couple more minutes," Chris called back.

"You heard me," she said more sharply than she'd intended. "We need to go. Now."

"Was it something I said?" Dan's voice trailed her.

She turned to answer and found him standing just

inches from her, tall and dark but not at all imposing. Because she wanted to move forward, she took a giant step backward.

How could she explain that keeping her distance was for his good as well as hers? Even if she could risk getting close to someone, it couldn't be Dan. Not when she was even more secretive than his ex-fiancée.

"Oh, no. Not at all." She smiled to punctuate her denial. "It's just getting late, is all."

"It's nine o'clock," he pointed out.

"Chris goes to sleep at nine-thirty."

"Not in the summer." Chris trudged up to them. "That's only when we're having school." To Dan, he said, "We start at seven-thirty."

"I thought classes at Indigo Springs Elementary started later than that," Dan said.

"I don't go to school there," Chris said. "I do school with Jill."

Yet another nugget of information Jill would rather Chris had kept to himself. "I homeschool him."

Before Dan could even think about quizzing her over why a woman working multiple jobs didn't send her brother to public school, she said, "We owe you a great big thank-you for helping us with Tinkerbell. Isn't that right, Chris?"

"Yeah." He cast another longing look at Tinkerbell. "Thank you, Dan."

"Any time." Dan spoke directly to her brother. "I'm going to reset Tinkerbell's leg tomorrow. If you like, you can stop by the office and see her."

"That'd be great!" Chris said, his mood instantly improved.

Her brother repeated that sentiment so many times on the brief walk back home that Jill accepted the inevitable. She might be able to avoid Dan, but she couldn't keep her brother away from him.

"Do you think Dan will really let me help tomorrow?" Chris asked, chattering the way he often did when it was only the two of them. "He didn't seem mad when I dropped the flashlight."

"Of course he wasn't mad." Jill tamped down a surge of dismay that her brother was still wrestling with insecurities. "Everybody makes mistakes, honey. I've told you that a hundred times."

"I'd try real hard not to do anything else wrong," he said.

"Mistakes are normal," she repeated. "Nobody tries to make one, but we all do."

"Then you think he'll let me help?" Chris actually skipped a few steps, something he hadn't done even when she'd driven forty miles last weekend to a go-kart track. "That would be so cool."

"You like Dan, don't you?" she asked while she thought about how to introduce the next subject without dampening her brother's excitement.

"Yes," he said without hesitation.

"I like him, too." She took a deep breath, then glanced around even though the street was quiet and they were the only two people on the sidewalk. "But we need to be even more careful around the people we like. It's important nobody knows we're from Atlanta."

Chris gasped and covered his mouth with his hand. "I said we were from Georgia! I'm sorry, Jill. I'm so stupid. I forgot."

"You are *not* stupid." She put her arm around him in a half hug. "You're a smart, brave boy. Don't you ever forget that."

They walked a few more steps before he asked in a small, scared voice, "Are the police going to come get me and take me back?"

"No, of course not." Her chest ached at his childish conclusion, which wasn't as far-fetched as it should have been. "The police don't have reason to suspect anything. It's our job to keep it that way."

"How?" he asked in a voice so quiet she hardly heard him.

"By being careful," she said. "Remember what you're supposed to say if anyone asks why you're living with me?"

"I'm supposed to say it's the best place for me."

The answer was vague enough to dissuade further questions. "That's right. But it's best not to say anything at all about Georgia. Or South Carolina."

Asking him not to talk about homeschooling would be piling it on too thick. She hadn't enrolled Chris in public school in case the P.I. had a way of searching enrollment.

"Can you do that, Chris?" she asked.

He nodded silently, the enthusiasm he'd been brimming with a moment ago gone, his steps slower.

She hated having to remind her brother to be careful, even more than she regretted being the antithesis of the kind of woman Dan should date.

It couldn't be helped, however. Their father was looking for Chris, and she would continue to do her damnedest to make sure he didn't find him.

MARK JACOBI KEPT the edger in his hands steady on Wednesday morning. He ignored the sweat that trickled down his back and gathered around his work goggles as well as the dull pain in his heart that never completely went away.

He concentrated instead on trimming the grass around the circular driveway that was constructed from concrete pavers set in a fussy pattern. The pretentious driveway was one of the many reasons he shouldn't have bought the property.

It led to a sprawling modern house with an elaborate entranceway, oversize bay windows and a backyard pool that came complete with a miniature waterfall. Everything about the house was too big, too ornate and too far away from his old neighborhood.

On the plus side, and this was a very big plus, living here made Arianne happy.

He was facing the general direction of the house, so he saw the garage door slide open, revealing his three-year-old Lexus and the new model Mercedes that Arianne drove.

She came into view, and for an instant he couldn't breathe. She was fifteen years younger than his fifty-four, but could have easily passed for thirty. She wore a pale-pink-and-white sleeveless dress that showed off her golden tan and her long legs, made to look longer still by strappy high-heeled sandals. The honey highlights in her shoulder-length brown hair caught the sun as she came toward him.

Damn, his wife was a beautiful woman.

Her makeup, not that she needed any, was perfect. Pink lipstick that made her lips glisten and eye makeup that caused eyes she said were too small to appear larger.

She covered her ears, prompting him to stop staring and switch off the motor. The neighborhood went abruptly silent.

"Well, that's better." She tilted her head, her brows coming together as she surveyed him. He felt a bead of sweat slide down his face. "Are you sure about not hiring a lawn service? I hate that you're spending a vacation day on yard work."

"I'm tougher than I look," he joked. The truth of the matter was that even with his six-figure salary they needed to save money somewhere with the rate of Arianne's spending. Besides, he enjoyed working in the yard. Sometimes it even helped take his mind off Jill and Chris. "Speaking of which, you look fantastic. Where are you headed?"

"Didn't I tell you?" She patted her already perfect hair into place. "There's a charity luncheon for the women's shelter at the Marriott."

She probably had told him, but Arianne was always heading off to one function or another. It was hard to keep all of them straight.

"I'm going to stick around here," Mark said, then lowered his voice even though there was no one else within sight. "That private investigator's supposed to call."

"He just did," Arianne said. "That's one of the things I came out here to tell you. You can call him back any time."

Mark had to fight not to rush for the house, so eager was he for the man he'd hired to help him put things right again. "Why didn't you get him to hold?"

"He doesn't have any news." Arianne's voice was equally soft, and he felt his chest deflate into what was now a familiar ache. There'd been no breaks in the case since they'd narrowly missed intercepting Jill and Chris in South Carolina. "Although maybe that's for the best."

"The best?" Mark could barely believe he'd heard her correctly. "How could you say that?"

"Oh, that came out all wrong." She bit her lower lip with her pretty, straight teeth. "All I meant is that Jill's better with Chris than I'll ever be. You know what a hard time he had warming up to me and how he tried his best to break us up."

"He's my son, Arianne," Mark said firmly. "He belongs with me."

"I know he does." She touched her chest and sighed softly. "Never mind what I said. Of course you feel that way. It was awful of Jill to run off with him like that. I still don't know what she was thinking."

Mark remembered his disbelief when Ray Williams, the guy Jill had been dating, phoned to say she was planning to pick up Chris from summer camp and leave town. The nightmare hadn't become real until a camp counselor confirmed his daughter had already come and gone.

"She was thinking she was protecting her brother." No matter the trouble Jill had caused him, Mark still had a hard time faulting her.

"Chris doesn't need protecting," Arianne said, not for the first time.

"I know that, and you know that." Mark didn't have to add that the social worker who'd investigated the case knew it, too. "Chris can be very persuasive when he wants to be."

"Jill must know he has a history of lying," Arianne said, covering ground they'd gone over before.

Chris was a good kid, but he'd been crying wolf since his mother's death. Mark had finally taken his son to a child psychologist, who explained that Chris was trying to get attention.

Mark loved his son and had tried his best to provide the attention he needed, but he was limited by the long hours he worked as a tax attorney.

"Jill and her brother have always been very close," Mark said. "She has a blind spot where he's concerned."

"She has one with me, too," Arianne said. "I wish she'd gotten to know me better so she could see how ridiculous those accusations are."

"When all this is over," Mark said, "we'll make sure she gets that opportunity."

Arianne gave him a tight smile. Jill and Chris had already been gone for almost a year. After that much time had passed, Arianne didn't think they could all become one big happy family. Mark, however, believed in miracles.

"I need to go," Arianne said, "but I'll be home in plenty of time to get ready for tonight."

"Tonight?"

"We have tickets to the symphony. Remember?"

With everything else that had been going on, he hadn't. He started to say he wasn't in the mood, but he could tell how much she was looking forward to it.

"I'll be ready," he said.

"I'll see you later, then." She leaned forward to kiss him, careful not to sully her expensive clothes against his sweat.

Her lips were warm and soft.

She turned away, hurrying toward the Mercedes on her high heels, her backside swaying temptingly.

The age difference had stopped him from proposing. So had the fact that he was a single father who'd already been divorced once and widowed once. But he hadn't been able to refuse when she'd asked him to marry her, especially because she knew he and Chris were a package deal. That had been two years ago and he'd felt like the luckiest man alive.

Maybe he shouldn't have been surprised when his luck had run out, yet he was.

It still seemed incredible that Jill could possibly believe Arianne had regularly locked Chris in a closet and threatened to kill him if he told anyone about it.

CHAPTER FIVE

"THAT WAS WAY COOL. Did you see me paddling the
rapids? Whoosh! I was awesome! Didn't you think I
was awesome?"

A young boy about the same age as Chris ambushed
Jill early on Wednesday afternoon when she exited the
supply room at the warehouse-type building that housed
Indigo River Rafters. The boy had been the most enthu-
siastic member of the group of white-water rafters Jill
had led down the river.

Although the trip had ended thirty minutes before
and most of the adventurers were already gone, the boy's
parents were at the counter paying for some souvenir
T-shirts.

"I most certainly did think you were awesome," Jill
said. "You beat those rapids to a pulp!"

"They didn't stand a chance," he agreed, his head
bobbing.

"Not a one," she said.

She wasn't about to diminish his pride by telling
him summer was the tamest time of year for riding the
rapids, aside from the special dam-release weekends
when the water level was deliberately raised to give a
boost to the fishing and rafting industries.

She'd explained as much to Chris, however, and he
still insisted white water rafting was too scary. Her latent

anger at her father's new wife briefly bubbled to the surface. What Arianne had done to her brother's psyche was criminal.

"Next time I want to go on one of those little boats like you had." The boy was referring to the single-person kayak Jill and the other guides used. "My parents were slowing me down."

"Liam. We're leaving!" the boy's father called from across the shop.

"Bye!" Liam said, then dashed across the store, his arms extended from his sides, as though he were flying.

"Energetic little guy, isn't he?" Annie Whitmore came around the counter and joined her, her blond hair stuffed into the twin of the Indigo River Rafters hat that Jill wore. "Probably runs his parents ragged. I wouldn't have the stamina to keep up with him."

Jill squashed the urge to tell Annie she wished Chris had half the boy's energy. He had once upon a time, even though he'd never been the boisterous type. She couldn't say anything of the sort, of course. It would bring up too many questions she couldn't answer.

"Sure, you would," Jill said. "You keep up with your daughter."

"Lindsey is a fifteen-year-old girl who loves to listen to her iPod and text her friends. She only expends unusual amounts of energy at the mall." Annie's voice was indulgent, the same way it was whenever she talked about her daughter.

"Speaking of Lindsey," Annie continued, "she was in here earlier and pointed out something mighty interesting."

"What's that?" Jill asked.

Annie marched over to the bulletin board near the exit and pointed to the notice Jill had posted that morning. "This. You can't leave until you tell me what it's about."

"And here I thought that posting was self-explanatory," Jill said.

"'Found—Caramel-colored female goat. Approximately one year old and two feet tall.'" Annie read the notice, her hands balanced on her slim hips. "Girl, that only brings up more questions."

"Only because you left out the important part." Jill pointed with her index finger to the word her friend had skipped over. "It's a *pygmy* goat."

"That clears it right up," Annie said. "I find a freakishly small goat myself every so often."

Jill laughed. When she'd first met Annie, the other woman had been shy to the point of being withdrawn. No longer. Either marriage, motherhood or a combination of the two had brought her true personality forth. In the past year Annie had married her high school love, been reunited with the daughter they'd put up for adoption when they were teenagers and gotten rid of the port-wine stain on her face that must have fueled some of her previous self-doubt.

"Dan says lots of people keep pygmy goats as pets," Jill said. "It seems like this one was a pet, too, except she's blind in one eye. That could be why somebody dumped her on the side of the road."

"How awful!" Annie exclaimed before her face scrunched up. "Wait a minute. Dan? Do you mean Dan Maguire? The vet?"

Jill cleared her throat. "Yes."

"Oh, my gosh! He left a message for you when you were out on the river and I didn't put two and two together."

"What are you talking about?" Jill asked warily.

"You and the hunky vet! Penelope told me she was fixing you two up. I can't believe one of her matches took!" Annie's voice carried throughout the shop. Thank goodness there was no one present but the two of them.

"You've got it wrong." Jill raised both hands palm sides up.

"Penelope didn't fix you up?"

"Well, yes," Jill said. "Except it *didn't* take. I was only with Dan last night because Tinkerbell has a broken leg."

Annie's nose wrinkled. "Tinkerbell?"

"The goat. Our best guess is a car sideswiped her and kept on going," Jill said. "Tinkerbell managed to walk into the woods, probably on adrenaline, until she collapsed. My brother found her. He came and got me, and I got Dan."

"Poor Tinkerbell," Annie said before her brow knitted. "But if that's all there is between you and Dan, why did he leave you that message?"

Jill had returned his call as soon as she'd gotten off the river, even before they'd stacked the rafts and put away the paddles.

"Dan called with an update on Tinkerbell." He'd also mentioned Chris had been waiting with Felicia outside the vet's office that morning before it opened. "Stanley

Kownacki knows of a farmer who raises pygmy goats. He offered to take her."

Annie frowned. "And here I thought you'd gotten yourself a hot boyfriend."

Jill couldn't help but smile. "Why is everybody so concerned about my love life?"

"Maybe because you don't have one?" Annie's question was rhetorical.

"Ha, ha," Jill said.

"Before you go, I need to tell you about the call I got today from our new mayor," Annie said. She was speaking of Charlie Bradford, who'd been elected last November in a special election after the previous mayor was unable to finish his term due to poor health. "You don't mind if I straighten up as we talk, do you?"

"I'll help." Jill walked with Annie to a shelf containing bottles of suntan lotion and insect repellent in no discernible order. "So what's up with Charlie? Did he tell you any jokes?"

"A quote, not a joke," Annie said. "Something about a lie traveling halfway around the world while the truth was putting on its shoes."

"Teresa says politics have given him a whole new source of material," Jill said, referring to Charlie's wife. She'd become acquainted with the couple during the spring festival and liked them immensely, especially Charlie, partly because he was so delightfully corny.

"Charlie was actually calling about something serious." Annie picked up a bottle of Coppertone that had fallen on the floor and placed it back on the shelf. "He knows I rent out mountain bikes and wanted to fill me in on a race called the Poconos Challenge."

"I've heard of it," Jill said slowly.

"Oh, good. Then you'll be up to speed when Charlie contacts you."

"Why would Charlie call me?" Jill asked.

"He's looking for a cyclist to present the proposal to the nominating committee." Annie stood back and surveyed the straightened shelf, apparently satisfied. "I told him he should try you."

"I don't think—"

The phone rang, interrupting Jill.

"I've got to get that." Annie moved toward the counter, talking as she went. "No one else is around today. My dad's got the day off, although I had to twist his arm to get him to take it." She picked up on the third ring, answering, "Indigo River Rafters."

Annie's smile grew wide as she listened to the caller. "You sure can talk to her, Dan," she said, her twinkling eyes on Jill. "She's right here."

She covered the mouthpiece and held out the phone to Jill, her eyebrows shifting up and down. "He sure does call a lot for a man who's not interested in you," she said in a loud whisper.

Darned if Jill's heartbeat didn't speed up.

She took the phone, avoiding looking at Annie. "Hey, Dan."

"We've got a problem," he said. "Your brother overheard me talking to that farmer about Tinkerbell. Now Chris is missing and so is the goat."

THE QUAINT DOWNTOWN of Indigo Springs, with its array of businesses that catered to families, afforded a lot of places for a ten-year-old boy to hide.

Add in a half-blind pygmy goat with its leg in a cast and that changed things.

Dan figured he and Jill should have located the pair in about five minutes flat. It had been twice that long since he'd met Jill in front of the vet's office, and so far they had no leads.

They spotted the bored-looking man sitting in the shade on a park bench outside a Main Street boutique at about the same time. From his seat, the man had a panoramic view of the downtown street where tourists strolled past restaurants, specialty shops and art galleries.

Jill reached him first, approaching with a smile, as she had every other person they'd questioned. She wore an Indigo River Rafters ball cap, quick-dry shorts, a T-shirt and old tennis shoes, yet still managed to look beautiful.

"Sorry to bother you," she said in her unhurried drawl, "but we're looking for a ten-year-old boy—"

"He hasn't been found yet?" the man interrupted, his heavy dark eyebrows arching. He crossed his arms over his barrel chest. "He's been missing for a good while."

"Pardon me for asking, but how do you know how long he's been missing?" Jill asked.

"I've been sitting here waiting for my wife to finish her shopping for what seems like forever. A fellow came by—" the man paused and scratched his chin "—oh, must have been a half hour ago and showed me a photo."

Jill's hand flew to her throat. Her face paled. "A man showed you a photo of Chris?"

Deep wrinkles appeared in the man's forehead. "I

don't think that was the boy's name. Or maybe it was. This old brain doesn't work as well as it used to."

Neither of them had been especially alarmed up to this point, assuming Chris was trying to elude them. Now Jill's breaths came so hard, Dan could hear them. He took a step closer to her, placing a hand on her back. She was trembling.

"The boy in the photo," Dan asked. "Did he have curly brown hair and brown eyes?"

He felt Jill's body tense as the man considered the question. "Brown hair, yes, but I don't know about the curly part. He was about...hey, there's the guy."

He pointed to a wiry, middle-aged man walking down the sidewalk on the other side of the street. The man was accompanied by a woman and a tall, skinny kid with long, straight brown hair. The kid's eyes were downcast and his hands shoved into the pockets of his worn jeans. Still, it was obvious he was in his early teens.

"We found him," the man yelled, waving to the guy on the bench.

"Dad, you're embarrassing me." The kid's comment was audible from across the street, even with the light midday traffic passing by.

"That the boy you're looking for?" the man on the bench asked.

"No," Jill said.

Dan felt the tension leave her body and wondered why she was so relieved. Her brother, after all, was still missing. "Like Jill said, the boy we're looking for is only ten."

"Guess that boy's older," the man said. "I couldn't see his face real good with that hair in his eyes."

"Chris is a lot shorter than that boy," Dan said. "He'd also be with a pygmy goat with a cast on its leg."

"A goat, you say?" The man chuckled. "Nope. Haven't seen either of them."

"You sure about that?" Jill asked. "Chris is wearing a white T-shirt and dark blue shorts. He looks a lot like me."

"Lady," the man said, "I might not have noticed the boy, but no way would I miss a crippled goat."

"He has a point," Dan remarked after they thanked the man and left. He moved his hand from her back to her shoulder and gave a gentle squeeze. "Don't worry. I'm sure Chris is fine. It's the middle of the afternoon, and Indigo Springs is a safe place."

"I know that," she said. The sun shone on her face, illuminating the faint worry lines around her eyes and mouth. "It's just that you read so many stories nowadays about child predators. I thought maybe some weirdo was going around secretly photographing kids."

"Unless he was a pretty dumb weirdo, it seems unlikely he'd be showing photos of the kids around town," Dan said.

"Yeah, I guess you're right," she said. "I overreacted."

"Perfectly understandable." Dan had learned from experience that emotions didn't always make sense when they involved a loved one. "What I don't understand is how your brother gave us the slip. Like the man said, that goat's an attention getter."

He looked through the glass front window of an ice cream parlor as they passed, spotting neither Chris nor Tinkerbell. No surprise there. He couldn't think of a single business in town, aside from his own, that would welcome a goat.

"Felicia said she'd call if Chris showed up at home." Jill's Southern drawl was more pronounced than usual. "So where do you suppose he is? We've been from one end of town to the other, and nothing."

"It's my fault," Dan said. "If I'd checked to see if Chris was listening to my phone call, we wouldn't be in this situation."

"You don't know that," Jill said gently. "Chris would have found out sooner or later that farmer was coming to pick up Tinkerbell."

"Then I should have figured out Chris would pull something like this."

"How?" Jill laid a hand on his arm. Her eyes, when they touched on his, were gentle and without reproach. She smelled of shampoo and river water, a surprisingly agreeable combination. "I'm his sister and I couldn't have predicted this."

Her comment didn't make him feel particularly better.

"Stop beating yourself up," she said. "Like you said, we just need to figure out where a boy could hide a goat."

They resumed walking, her shorter, quicker steps perfectly in sync with his slower, measured gait.

"Maybe Chris isn't hiding." Dan spoke his thoughts aloud. "Maybe he went to a friend's house."

"I'm afraid Chris doesn't have any friends," Jill said. "At least, not any he'd feel comfortable visiting."

"Haven't you and Chris lived here for a while?"

"We have." She paused, as though searching for

words. "It's just that Chris is, well, shy. With the home-schooling, he's not around kids his age."

Not for the first time, Dan wondered at her reasons for homeschooling her brother. If he hadn't been aware of the seconds ticking by, he would have pointed out there were other social outlets. Like sports teams and Boy Scouts.

"How about *your* friends, then?" Dan asked.

"I don't think so," she said slowly. "Chris usually stays home when I visit friends. About the only time I got him to come with me was when… Oh, my gosh! I bet that's where he is!"

They'd reached a street corner. Instead of crossing, she made a ninety-degree turn and walked quickly toward a residential neighborhood of manicured lawns and grand old houses.

"Care to tell me where we're going?" he asked as he kept up with her.

"Sorry." She was practically jogging. "Do you know Annie Whitmore?"

"Sure," he said. "She's married to the doctor. Their daughter Lindsey brings her dog, Hobo, to the office."

"Then you probably know Lindsey moved to town at the beginning of the summer to live with Annie and Ryan."

Dan nodded. He wasn't certain of all the details, but he was aware that Lindsey had been adopted as a baby and that the Whitmores were her biological parents.

"Well, I got Felicia to give me her recipe for double chocolate chip cookies and brought a plate over to welcome Lindsey to town."

"And Chris came with you," Dan guessed.

Jill turned up a sidewalk to the most impressive house on the street, a sprawling Colonial with yellow siding. The lawn surrounding it was of stunning perfection. The flower beds hugging the house were awash with color.

"He did," Jill confirmed. "He and Lindsey hit it off. She taught him how to play Guitar Hero."

"Guitar what?"

"It's a video game, darlin'. All the young people…" She abruptly stopped talking and grabbed his arm, her lips curving into a smile. She wore no makeup, her skin was slightly sunburned and the sun made the freckles on her nose stand out. She'd never looked better. "Did you hear that?"

He nodded. "Sounded like a bleat to me."

They followed the sound around the house to a back-yard filled with more flowers, green shrubs and tall oak trees. Chris and Lindsey had their backs toward them, completely engrossed in the antics of the pygmy goat. Tinkerbell pushed an inflated beach ball with her nose, waited for the ball to settle, then ran after the ball to nudge it again.

Dan felt a surge of pride that the animal was getting along just fine on its mending leg.

Lindsey spotted them first, her pretty face breaking into a welcoming smile. "Jill! Dr. Maguire! You have got to come over here and watch Chris's goat!"

Chris turned around then, too, his expression not nearly as welcoming. Tinkerbell did a one-eighty when the wind blew the beach ball in an unexpected direction. Lindsey laughed delightedly.

"He's so cute I can't stand it," Lindsey said. "If I

didn't have Hobo, I'd beg my mom and dad to get me a pygmy goat, too."

"Tinkerbell doesn't belong to Chris." Jill strolled up to the girl, slanting her brother a pointed look. "Isn't that right, Chris?"

Chris said nothing, staring sullenly at the ground. There was something about him that was so vulnerable Dan couldn't help but empathize with him.

"Really?" Lindsey asked. "Then whose goat is she?"

"We don't know," Dan said. "We think someone dumped her on the side of the road, but it's possible she's a pet that got loose."

"Then she doesn't live in a crate inside Chris's bedroom?" Lindsey asked.

"Of course not," Jill said. "Some people keep pygmy goats as pets, but they don't live in houses. They're more like farm animals."

"Tinkerbell doesn't want to go to some dumb old goat farm." Chris thrust out his lower lip. "She wants to come home with me."

"She can't, Chris," Jill said gently. She obviously didn't have it in her heart to be angry at him any more than Dan did. "You know Mrs. Feldman doesn't have anywhere to put her."

"Then why can't she stay with Dan like last night?" Chris asked. "Then I could come visit her."

"We talked about this, Chris." Dan pitched his voice the same low tone as Jill's. "The Humphreys raise pygmy goats. They make a point of never selling just one. Goats are social animals that aren't happy unless they have company."

"I can keep Tinkerbell company!" Chris cried.

Jill went to her brother and put a hand on his shoulder. "I know how you feel about Tinkerbell, but she has to go to the farm."

"She can't." Chris sounded triumphant. "It's way past four o'clock."

"That's when Humphrey was supposed to pick up Tinkerbell," Dan explained. He put a hand on Chris's free shoulder so both he and Jill were bracing the boy for the blow to come. "I called the farmer and told him we'd bring Tinkerbell to the farm."

"No!" Chris cried, shaking off their hands.

"You heard Dan about how goats like to be with other goats," Jill said. "The farm is the best place for her."

Chris's shoulders slumped.

"Tell you what, Chris." Dan met Jill's eyes over her brother's head, hoping he wasn't stepping over any lines. "You can come with me. That way you can check out the farm and make sure Tinkerbell will be happy there."

Jill mouthed a silent *Thank you*.

"All three of us can go," Jill said. "That is, if Dan doesn't mind."

Was she kidding? Dan would seize on any excuse to spend time with her, even though his intention had been to ease Chris's distress.

"Of course you can come," Dan said. "Lindsey can, too, if she'd like."

"Thanks, but my mom and dad are taking me to that new pizza place." Lindsey looked from Dan to Jill. "You two should go there some time. I hear it's a cool date place."

"We just might do that." Dan kind of liked the idea. "Thanks for the tip."

"But we—" Jill began.

"Need to get going," Dan interrupted. "We want to get Tinkerbell settled with plenty of time before it gets dark."

IF JILL HAD BEEN a pygmy goat, she doubted she could have resisted the Tiny Treasures Farm.

From a cursory glance, it looked like any of the other farms nestled in the valleys of the Pocono Mountains. A detached farmhouse with red siding and white awnings was positioned to the right of a long gravel driveway. To its left was a medium-sized red barn surrounded by a fenced area.

Only upon closer inspection did the differences become apparent. Between the barn and the house was an odd playground equipped with old tires, boulders, wooden cable spools and lots and lots of little goats.

Fifteen, by Jill's count. All of them scampering and playing in the waning sun as though they were at the best place on earth.

All of them, that is, except Tinkerbell. The goat had been glued to her brother's side since they'd taken her out of the crate they'd used to transport her.

"Tinkerbell doesn't like it here," Chris stated sullenly.

"Give her a chance, honey." Jill couldn't be angry at Chris about his lies and his disappearing act when his heart was obviously breaking. She'd eventually make her displeasure known and stress to him it was important she know where he was at all times, but not now. "We just got here. She needs time to get accustomed to her surroundings."

"That's exactly right." Mr. Humphrey, one of the owners of Tiny Treasures Farm, was a big man in his seventies with massive shoulders, bushy eyebrows and a florid, friendly face. "You're one sharp cookie, Jill. No wonder Dan married you."

First Lindsey had assumed she and Dan were dating, and now this. Dan was just inches from her, where she could smell the pleasant scent of soap, shampoo and man. She increased the space between them.

"Dan and I aren't married," Jill said.

"Give it time," Mr. Humphrey advised. "Some men are slow to pop the question. I should know. Took me a while myself after I met my wife."

"But we're not—"

"Let me show you 'round the place." Mr. Humphrey seemed not to notice her attempt to correct his misconception. He strode across the grassy enclosure without looking back, as though he fully expected them to follow.

Dan cocked one eyebrow at her, then headed after the farmer, as silent as the sleeping tomcat stretched out under the picnic table. Come to think of it, he hadn't said a word to correct Lindsey, either.

Jill fell into step beside Dan. "Why didn't you tell Mr. Humphrey we weren't dating?" she asked in a quiet voice.

"He didn't listen to you," Dan said. "What makes you think I'd have any better luck?"

She had to admit that made sense. "I just can't figure out why everyone keeps making that same mistake."

"It's kind of flattering." Dan smiled at her. Today he wore a short-sleeved casual shirt that showed off the musculature in his arms. The wind blew through his dark hair, lending him a dashing quality. "If someone as pretty as you were dating me, I'd be doing something right."

Warmth spread through Jill, although the sun was no longer particularly bright.

"Over here's the barn," Mr. Humphrey bellowed, interrupting the moment.

Dan's eyes gleamed. "We'd better catch up."

Mr. Humphrey didn't break his long, boot-propelled strides, not seeming to notice they weren't directly behind him. "Inside are the stalls where the goats hunker down for the night."

This was something Chris should see, too. She half turned as she walked, discovering her brother was rooted to the spot where they'd left him. He was rubbing Tinkerbell's snout, the way he'd discovered the goat liked. Even beside the miniature animal, Chris looked small and sad.

"Chris?" she called. "Are you coming, honey?"

He shook his head. Resigned, she continued on to the barn.

"My wife—she's away visiting her mother—treats the pygmies better than she does me," Mr. Humphrey said when the three of them were inside a tidy barn that smelled of hay and grass. "I help her out on occasion, but this is her enterprise."

He gestured to a row of stalls with open doors as he led them the length of the barn.

"The pygmies usually stay two to a stall," Mr.

Humphrey said. "We keep their hay and their water elevated. They don't like eating where they sleep."

He proceeded to outline a day in the life of one of his wife's "little darlin's," as he said she called them. Their regime consisted primarily of eating, playing and sleeping.

"She tells customers her goats are as tame and affectionate as they come, although between you and me we occasionally get an ornery one." Mr. Humphrey delivered the last comment in a lowered voice after they'd made a loop of the property and were heading back toward Chris. "When we sell 'em, she makes sure the pygmies go to good homes. Our customers are in the market for pets. She makes real sure her little darlin's don't go to any butchers."

"Butchers!" Chris exclaimed, tears welling in his eyes. He hugged Tinkerbell hard around the neck. "You sell your goats to butchers!"

"No, honey," Jill refuted. "Mr. Humphrey said his wife makes sure *not* to sell the goats to butchers. The animals they raise here have good lives."

Chris loosened his grip on Tinkerbell's neck. His lower lip, however, still trembled.

"Fantastic lives. The does are breeding machines, but my wife sees to it they only have one pregnancy a year. She waits till they're at least eighteen months old to breed 'em." Mr. Humphrey bent at the waist and started to put out his hand to Tinkerbell, then withdrew it. "Something wrong with her left eye?"

"She's blind in that eye," Dan said. "Didn't notice it myself at first."

Mr. Humphrey sucked in a breath through his teeth.

"That's gonna change things. The wife's goats, they're all up to NPGA standards."

"NPGA?" Jill asked.

"National Pygmy Goat Association," Mr. Humphrey explained. "She prides herself on turning out animals that are a credit to their breed. She'd never breed this one. Or put her up for sale, either."

Unease skittered through Jill. They all knew it was extremely unlikely Tinkerbell's original owner would materialize and reclaim her, despite the feelers they'd put out. "Then what'll happen to her?"

Chris positioned himself between the pygmy goat and the farmer, as though he meant to defend her.

"We can't afford to have her around our studs in case that blindness of hers is genetic," Mr. Humphrey said. "We don't milk our goats here, but other breeders do. My wife could ask around to see if anyone else will take her."

"You mean Tinkerbell will never be a pet?" Chris asked.

"The goat's half blind, son. And I'm thinking hair might not grow back where that abrasion is," Mr. Humphrey said, not unkindly. "My wife's worked hard to develop this farm's reputation. She can't afford to be selling substandard animals."

"Tinkerbell has standards!" Chris objected.

Mr. Humphrey cocked his head. "What?"

"He's trying to say the goat would make a good pet," Dan translated.

"Maybe she would, but our customers wouldn't want her. Not when they can have perfection." Mr. Humphrey gestured to the pygmy goats on the makeshift playground.

"Tinkerbell's better than any of those stupid goats," Chris said. "Tell him, Jill."

"Tinkerbell's a fine goat," Jill said lamely.

"We don't have to leave her here, do we?" Chris pleaded. "We can take her back home with us?"

Tears brimmed in her brother's eyes, nearly breaking Jill's heart. Chris had already had too many disappointments in his young life. She hated to deal him another.

"You know there isn't any place for her at Mrs. Feldman's," Jill said.

"But you heard him," Chris said. "He's going to give Tinkerbell to someone who'll use her for milk!"

"Goats don't mind being milked, son," Mr. Humphrey said. "It's natural."

"Tinkerbell doesn't want to stay here!" Chris said. "I know she doesn't!"

Jill searched her brain for something she could say to calm her brother and came up blank. Her eyes flew to Dan. He nodded at her, as though he had everything under control.

"Tinkerbell doesn't have to stay here, Chris," Dan said. "I'll keep her."

Even as relief spread through Jill and her brother's tears started to dry, she recognized that they had put Dan in a terrible position. He couldn't possibly want a goat.

"We couldn't ask you to do that," she said.

"You didn't ask. I offered."

"But didn't you say goats need companions?" It

wouldn't be fair to him if she didn't point out the drawbacks. "Isn't that one of the reasons you contacted Mr. Humphrey?"

"It is," Dan confirmed. "That's why I'm buying another goat to keep Tinkerbell company."

CHAPTER SIX

JILL WIPED AT THE spill on the bar the next night, moving the rag over the surface so quickly she missed a spot and had to do it over again. She hung the rag up in its usual place, then nearly plowed into Chuck Dudza.

"You sure are in a rush to get out of here tonight." Chuck himself never seemed to be in a hurry, even when the bar he owned was at its busiest. He had a knack for carrying on a leisurely conversation while he filled one drink order after another. Jill liked to think that was also one of her strong points. "Got plans?"

"Not really." Jill didn't have plans in the traditional sense. "I'm just eager for some fresh air, is all."

"We've had slow nights many a time and you usually offer to stay and close up," Chuck pointed out. Darn the man. He was always complaining about how his memory had started to fail when he hit sixty, yet he was sharper than she was.

"You already said you'd close up tonight," Jill said. "Might I remind you that you're the one who told me to go home."

"Didn't expect you to accept so quick."

"I don't get home before midnight very often. I was thinking I could read a little before I went to sleep," Jill said. "I'm in the middle of *All Creatures Great and Small,* and it's hard to put down."

"Isn't that book about a vet?"

Jill made sure to take Chris to the library at least once a week, during which time she fed her own reading habit. She usually chose popular fiction, but this week she'd wandered the nonfiction aisles until the old classic had caught her interest.

"Yes," she said. "A country vet in Yorkshire, England. The book was written almost forty years ago."

"Interesting you're reading about a vet." Chuck grinned. "Would your hurry to get out of here have anything to do with Dan Maguire?"

"Of course not." Jill felt heat rise to her face. Great. Now Chuck would never believe her.

"I heard you ate at that new pizza place with him last night," Chuck said.

"We got takeout," Jill corrected. "And it's not what you think. Chris was waiting in the car with Tinkerbell and Bluebell."

"Who the heck are Tinkerbell and Bluebell?"

"Dan's pygmy goats." Jill moved in a circular pattern while she answered, maneuvering her body so the bar owner was no longer between her and the exit. "Chris has taken a real shine to them. That's why we were with Dan last night."

Chuck winked broadly at her. "If you say so."

"I do." She ignored the wink as she backed away from him. Arguing with Chuck when he got something in his head never did any good. "I've got tomorrow night off, but I'll see you Saturday."

"Have fun," he called after her.

The air outside had cooled with nightfall, one of the

perks of living in Indigo Springs. Back in Atlanta, the nights were often as warm and as humid as the days.

She headed in the general direction of home, changing her usual route slightly so she'd pass by Dan's house. They hadn't arranged an assignation, as Chuck seemed to think. She simply wanted to thank Dan in person for the incredibly kind thing he'd done.

She'd searched for the right moment to offer her thanks last night, but it had never come. From the time Dan had purchased the second goat and they'd loaded the animals into his truck, the night had passed in a whirlwind of activity. They'd barely had time to scarf down the pizza.

But now here she was, on the street where Dan lived, with the goats presumably asleep, the same way her brother should be.

Dan's house was a modest, one-story ranch with a neat lawn and decent curb appeal. The porch light shone like a beacon. The rest of the house was dark except for a glow coming from a room on the far left side.

Probably Dan's bedroom.

She wondered if he slept in pajamas, boxer shorts or nothing at all. The night suddenly felt warmer.

"This was a bad idea, Jacobi," Jill muttered to herself.

Of course Dan was getting ready to go to sleep. It was past eleven o'clock and the vet's office opened by nine. If she rang his doorbell now, he'd think she was there for more than a thank-you.

She was under a streetlight, the worst place if Dan should happen to look out the window. She was about to cross to the opposite side of the street when she heard a motorized sound. Dan's garage door opened slowly, revealing feet in slides, hair-sprinkled legs left bare beneath a pair of gym shorts, a lean torso covered by a T-shirt, then Dan's handsome face.

The shorts and T-shirt instantly became tied with nothing at all in her speculation over what he wore to bed.

He started dragging a rubber trash can on wheels to the curb. Her feet felt as though they were stuck in wet cement. She got them loose and tried to jump back into the shadows.

"Jill?" he called. "Is that you?"

She grimaced. Her only choice was to step forward into the full glow of a streetlight. She affected a casual pose and a smile, as though she'd run into him in the full light of day. "Hey, Dan."

"Hi, Jill." He finished hauling the can to the curb, then walked toward her. Although Dan looked great in his work clothes, she preferred him this way. The man really did have a set of gorgeous legs. "What are you doing out here?"

That was easy enough to answer. "Walking home from the Blue Haven. I got off early tonight."

"Isn't this a few blocks out of your way?"

No use denying what anyone with a sense of direction could figure out. "Yes. Yes, it is."

She shifted from foot to foot, listening to the cries of the cicadas reach a slow crescendo. He said nothing, waiting.

"Okay. You caught me," she said. "I'm here because of you."

The darkness enveloping them lent the situation an

air of intimacy and her comments the heavy hint of suggestion. She chewed on her bottom lip. "I didn't mean that the way it sounded."

"How do you think it sounded?" His gaze didn't leave her face.

"Like I saw that light in your bedroom window and got ideas," she said.

"Did you get ideas?"

Before Jill had plotted to go into hiding with Chris, she'd made it a point to tell the truth. She hated that circumstances had forced her to become a decent liar. Occasionally, however, the skill came in handy.

"I got the idea it was too late to bother you." There. Technically that wasn't even a lie. She'd simply neglected to tell him the entire truth.

"Bother me?" Was it her imagination or did his question have sexual undertones? "About what?"

Jill almost groaned. What was the matter with her that she read innuendo into the simplest of questions? She wanted to cry with the cicadas.

"About the goats," she said. "I didn't get a chance last night to properly thank you for the wonderful thing you did for Chris. I nearly called you a dozen times today, but this seemed like something I should say in person."

He shrugged. "I didn't do much."

"You must be kidding me." She took a step closer to him, remembering how he'd come to the rescue. "You've got two pygmy goats in your backyard."

"I'm a vet," he said. "I'm used to having animals around."

"Maybe so. But if it weren't for Chris, you wouldn't

have any goats." She had to tilt her head to gaze up at him. "Let me reimburse you for what Bluebell cost. I can also chip in for their upkeep."

"Thanks, but no thanks," he said in a tone that brooked no argument.

"I promise you I won't forgot this," Jill said. "If you ever need a favor, all you have to do is let me know."

"You don't owe me anything. I like Chris." He reached out and captured her hand. Warmth instantly spread through her. "I like his sister, too."

Her throat suddenly felt parched. She swallowed, wondering why she was leaving her hand where it was.

"Tell you what, if you're set on paying me back, come inside," he invited. "I'll open a bottle of wine and we can talk, get to know each other better."

Panic flared inside her, and she shook her head. "That's not a good idea."

"Whoa," he said. "I didn't mean to make you uncomfortable. You can trust me, if that's what you're worried about. All I'm asking for is wine and conversation."

She met his eyes, perfectly visible in the moonlight. She believed he wouldn't push her to sleep with him, yet she *couldn't* trust him. Not with any meaningful conversation. Not after she'd been burned twice by people she had faith in.

Her heart jerked and started. She wouldn't talk of her past if she went inside the house with him. She was less sure of her resolve to stay out of his bed. How had this happened? How had she come by for such an innocent reason and gotten to this point?

"I can't." She cast about for a sensible excuse, but her brain felt scrambled with him touching her. She drew her hand away from his. "I'm guiding a white-water trip early tomorrow. I need my sleep."

His lips quirked, his only sign of disappointment. "I bet it's beautiful in the mornings on the river."

Finally, a safe subject.

"The best time to kayak is before anyone is awake other than the herons and the eagles." Her trip tomorrow morning was at ten, a fact she'd conveniently neglected to tell him, but she sometimes went on short sleep when she kayaked for pleasure. "The sky is almost achingly blue and it's so quiet the rumble of the white water sounds like thunder."

"Forget what I said about not calling in a favor." His voice sounded soft and seductive in the darkness. "I just thought of one."

Her muscles clenched while she marveled at how easily he'd resurrected the sexual tension between them.

"You can give me a kayak lesson," he said.

She relaxed. "Are you serious?"

"Completely. You did say you owed me."

"Then you're on." This was more like what she'd had in mind. She mentally went over her weekend schedule. She was guiding trips Friday and Saturday mornings, bartending Saturday and Sunday nights and taking naps in between. "I'm free Sunday morning if I skip my bike ride. Say, at seven. Would that work for you?"

"Perfectly," he said.

She might have qualms about being alone with Dan in a darkened house, but surely she could handle him on a sunny river.

STARSKY AND HUTCH CLAWED at the door leading to the back porch on Friday morning, whimpering and sending Dan pleading looks. Before the temperature rose on summer mornings, he liked to let the still-cool air flow through the window and door screens. He usually left the back door unlocked so the dogs could come and go into the fenced backyard. Not today.

"Forget it," Dan told the dogs. "You're not getting anywhere near those pygmy goats."

Introducing the dogs to his two newest pets, however, needed to become a priority. It had been a simple matter to keep the dogs out of the backyard that first night Tinkerbell had stayed in the shed. That wouldn't work now that the goats had become permanent residents.

Dan needed to find out whether the dogs would welcome the newcomers or try to tear them apart.

He'd rescued Starsky and Hutch, who were in the same litter, from an animal shelter back in Ohio. They were mutts, a mix of breeds that almost certainly included some Doberman. Since goats were prey animals and Dobermans hunters, it was entirely possible the dogs would attack.

The proper way to begin acclimatizing the animals was while the dogs were leashed. He'd try that tactic soon, but not this morning. He started work in thirty minutes.

His cell phone rang. He snatched it off the kitchen counter and checked caller ID. His oldest sister, who called occasionally but irregularly. He immediately clicked on the phone.

"Karen? Is everything all right?"

"Everything's fine." She had a strong authoritative

voice to go along with her personality. The firstborn of the four Maguire children, Karen had taken the role of the oldest to heart. Dan's father used to call her the Little General. "Is that Starsky and Hutch I hear? How are they?"

"In need of obedience school," he said.

She laughed. "How's their owner?"

"I can't complain." Dan peered out the kitchen window to see the two pygmy goats romping around the yard. He checked the fencing, reassuring himself it was high enough to leave them outside during the day. "Listen, Karen, I'd love to talk but I'm due at work soon. Any specific reason you're calling?"

"As a matter of fact, there is," she said. "Nancy told me you'd sent in your RSVP."

Now the call made sense. Their first cousin was planning a lavish wedding in late August at a local country club. She'd invited her entire family and all of the groom-to-be's relatives, including the groom's sister Maggie.

"I wish you'd change your mind about not coming," she said. "Nancy feels the same. You don't even have to call her. I'll do it for you."

Dan suppressed a sigh. "I'm not coming to the wedding, Karen."

"It's because of Maggie, isn't it?" Karen asked. "The best revenge would be to come and show her you've gotten over her."

He'd been striving to do exactly that for the past year.

"Just because I don't want to see Maggie—" and her

husband, he added silently "—doesn't mean I'm pining for her."

"It'll seem that way to her," she argued. "When are you going to realize she did you a favor?"

"She deceived me, Karen," he said softly even though the logical part of his mind had reached the same conclusion. "She knew she was leaving for an entire month and didn't say a word."

"Exactly. What kind of life would you have with someone who could lie to your face like that?"

"Not much of a life," Dan conceded.

"So when are you going to be ready to meet someone else?"

"Maybe I already have," he said without thinking.

"You're kidding! That's great!" his sister exclaimed. He closed his eyes, wishing he could rewind the conversation, bracing himself for what was coming. "You can bring her to the wedding."

"We barely know each other," Dan said. "We haven't even been—"

"You have almost two months to get better acquainted," Karen interrupted before he could say they had yet to go on a date. She hardly took a breath between sentences. "What's her name? How did you meet? What does she do for a living? Do you—?"

Raucous barking drowned out his sister's next question. The noise wasn't coming from the house but the yard. Dan's eyes flew to the screen door, which was standing wide open. He should have known the flimsy lock wouldn't hold with the dogs jumping against the door.

"I've gotta go, Karen." He disconnected the call,

dropped the phone and sprinted for the backyard. He was sickeningly aware he didn't have a prayer of arriving before the dogs.

He thundered down the porch steps, his bare feet slapping on the hard surface. He hit the dew-sprinkled grass so fast he slipped and almost went down.

Then he stopped dead.

The two goats stood perfectly still in the middle of the yard. Starsky and Hutch circled them, sniffing at the air, their tails pointing skyward.

His stomach plummeted as Starsky advanced, targeting Tinkerbell, the smaller of the two goats.

Except something was off. The dog wasn't approaching the goat's hindquarters, the area most vulnerable to an attack. Starsky was going straight at her, aiming for her…snout?

The dog had no sooner nudged Tinkerbell than she butted him back, as good as she'd gotten. She bleated a loud, angry cry, then stared him down.

Starsky retreated, his tail between his legs. Hutch took a few steps backward. Dan could breathe again.

Saved by the dog-and-goat show, he thought, but it was only a temporary reprieve. His sister would call back. Sooner or later he'd have to admit he wasn't dating anyone.

Unless, of course, the kayak lesson went according to plan.

THE LEHIGH RIVER EARLY on a summer morning was Jill's idea of paradise. The sun was warm on her back and the shimmering water so beautiful it made her throat ache.

She breathed in the invigorating scent of the river

water, as she'd done so many times before. Gazing up at the blue sky, she spotted an incredible sight—an eagle in flight.

She'd seen the eagle with its wings spread as it soared overhead only once before. She pointed skyward, eager to share her find.

"Do you see that?" she called.

"Incredible," Dan Maguire said, a grin splitting his face.

Jill usually jealously guarded her early-morning time on the river, getting pleasure in the isolation. This Sunday morning she was glad to have Dan along. The weather and the river had cooperated, the conditions perfect for a beginning kayaker.

She'd gone over the basics when he'd met her at Indigo River Rafters at 7:00 a.m. sharp to pick up the kayaks and transport them upriver.

Keep your hands a little more than a shoulder's width apart on the shaft of the paddle. Make sure the smooth, concave part faces you. Rotate your torso and extend your arms while taking a stroke on the right side of the kayak, then repeat on the left.

He'd followed her directions to the letter—not that kayaking in ideal conditions was difficult.

"The white water should be mild," she'd told him before they started. "It hasn't rained lately, so the river is fairly low. There's only one set of rapids that could give us trouble."

They were approaching those rapids now, affectionately known as Baby's Gurgles by the Indigo River Rafter guides. The growl of the water made her senses quicken, as they always did this close to rapids.

Last summer a boy had nearly drowned at Baby's Gurgles before being pulled from the water by a mysterious savior. Her friend Sara Brenneman had recently confided the modest hero was her fiancé, Michael Donahue, who was also Felicia's great-nephew. The circumstances on that day, however, had been vastly different, with the water level much higher and the flow substantially quicker.

Dan's kayak was even with hers. The water's roar made conversation difficult, so she gestured to him to suggest they veer left and avoid the rapid.

He shook his head, pointing straight ahead to indicate his desire to meet the challenge. His kayak shot in front of hers—not ideal, but not worrisome, either.

This rapid would probably be classified as a III on a scale of I to V, at best moderately difficult given today's conditions. With the proficiency Dan had already shown at kayaking, he should have no trouble.

The water bubbled around them with more force than Jill had anticipated. She spotted some rocks jutting above the surface and maneuvered her kayak to avoid them. Her boat slid over the water, the sensation not unlike that of the smaller ripples of a roller coaster.

She concentrated on driving her paddle through the water to guide her kayak around the rocks, silently congratulating herself for meeting the challenge. She looked up to check on Dan—and spotted his overturned kayak.

Her heart squeezed and panic clogged her throat. Exiting a kayak while underwater was notoriously difficult. She'd gone over the basics of rolling a kayak, but it was a tricky maneuver.

He could drown.

She thrust her paddle into the water, propelling her boat forward, desperate to reach him. She wasn't sure if the sting in her eyes was from the water or tears.

Then the overturned kayak rolled, the craft turning upright, the paddle slicing through the water with near-expert precision. She held her breath. Dan's head popped out of the river, water dripping down his face and torso.

Relief washed over her like white water over rocks, so great she almost didn't recognize the significance of his whoop.

The sound wasn't audible over the gurgling white water, but she could read his lips. The man had definitely whooped.

He could be happy to be alive, but she didn't think that was it. He appeared to be in his element. She'd bet her quick-dry shirt he was also no novice kayaker.

The rest of the trip passed swiftly. She looked for evidence to support her theory, finding it in the ease in which he navigated the next few rapids.

"That was some kayak roll," Jill remarked after she'd dragged her kayak out of the river at the spot near headquarters where all the Indigo River Rafters trips ended. "I don't think I've ever seen a first-timer do one of those."

Dan paused in the act of tipping his kayak over to empty it of the water that had accumulated during the trip.

"So you noticed I wasn't a beginner?" He winced. "In my defense, I didn't say I'd never kayaked before. I'm hardly an expert, either. It's been years since I've done it."

"And here I thought asking for a lesson was a pretty strong indication you were new to this." She emptied her own kayak, then set it on dry land. "Why would you mislead me like that?"

He righted his boat, positioned it next to hers, then straightened. His Ohio State baseball cap shielded his eyes from the sun and from her. If she hadn't been so annoyed, she might have admired how very good he looked in his shorts and T-shirt.

"Isn't it obvious?" Dan asked. "I'm trying to grow on you."

The water flowed gently here, creating only the softest of rumbles, but she knew she'd heard him correctly.

"Will you sit with me?" He indicated a large flat rock that overlooked the water. They were in sight of the building housing river raft headquarters where either Annie or her father would be getting ready for the day. Very soon, customers would start arriving for the morning trip. For now, though, all was relatively quiet.

She waited until he sat down, then did the same, careful to keep a body length between them. She both wanted to hear what he had to say and didn't.

"I had to get creative to spend time with you." He gave her a crooked, endearing grin, and she felt her heartbeat speed up. "I'm trying to ask you on a date."

Jill stifled the pleasure that threatened to burst forth. "You said you didn't want to date me."

"That was before I got to know you," he said. "The truth is I didn't want to date anyone after what my fiancée did. But most women aren't like her. You're not like her."

A few years ago, that had been the case. It wasn't any longer.

She took a deep breath and tried to sound firm. "The answer's still no."

He stared at her for a moment, then laid a hand on her cheek. Their gazes snagged as he very slowly and deliberately inched forward, giving her every opportunity to pull back. His lips touched hers in a soft kiss that still managed to send what felt like electricity shooting through her. And then it was over, before it had barely begun. He dropped his hand.

"Why did you do that?" she asked.

"So you couldn't deny you were attracted to me."

She finally broke eye contact and cast about for a truth she could share. "That's not the point. I meant what I said about this not being a good time for me to start dating. Chris and I, we're not in Indigo Springs to stay."

If she got the slightest notion her father's hired man was close, she'd pack up and not look back. Like Dan's ex-fiancée, she wouldn't say goodbye.

"Why?" he asked.

Of all the questions he could have asked, that was the most difficult to answer. She stumbled for a reply.

"I'm a Southerner at heart," she finally said. "Last winter was pretty rough. I'm not sure I'm up for another cold spell. Like I told you before, Chris hasn't made a lot of friends here, so it might be a good time to move."

"Might be? Does that mean you haven't made up your mind about leaving?"

"I haven't decided when we'll leave." She had little hope that she and Chris could successfully hide out in one place for much longer than they'd already been in Indigo Springs. "It could be very soon."

There, that sounded reasonably sensible.

"So now you understand why we can't date," she finished.

"Can't say that I do." He reached out and touched her arm, again managing to stir her with the barest of effort. "I think we should enjoy each other while you're still in town."

"But I could be here one day and gone the next," she said. "Just like your fiancée."

"You plan to pack up half the furniture in my house and leave town while I'm at work?" Dan's smile was bemused.

"Well, no," she said.

"Then why don't you let me decide what I can handle?"

She scooted backward on the rock so he could no longer touch her. "It's not only that. It's what I can handle, too. And I can't manage a relationship when my future's so uncertain."

He stared at her for a long time. She only hoped he wouldn't kiss her again, because she might let her very valid reason blow away with the warm wind tousling his dark hair.

"I only have one more question," he said.

She waited, holding her breath.

"When you and Chris leave town, you're taking those pygmy goats with you, right?"

She laughed, refusing to think about how much harder it was to resist a man with a sense of humor.

CHAPTER SEVEN

CHRIS JACOBI LICKED enthusiastically at his ice cream cone, then grinned at Dan.

"Double chocolate fudge brownie's the best!" he declared.

The rich, creamy flavor was also possibly the messiest. Chocolate ringed the boy's mouth, dotted his nose and had dribbled onto his T-shirt.

"Gotta disagree." Dan held up his own cone. "Pistachio nut can't be beat."

"No way!" Chris said.

It was evening, and they were in the downtown park around the corner from the ice cream parlor, sitting atop a picnic table with their feet resting on the bench seat.

Daylight had turned to dusk, which hadn't cut down on the activity in the park. Small children filled the playground and boys around Chris's age chased each other around an open field.

"Bart likes butterfinger swirl," Chris declared between passes at his ice cream cone. "He eats funny. He's real loud."

The days had settled into a pattern in the week and a half since Dan had purchased the pygmy goats. Chris stopped by to visit Tinkerbell and Bluebell while Dan was at work and then again after dinner.

Jill didn't want her brother walking home in the dark by himself, even though it was only a couple of blocks. On the nights she worked at the Blue Haven, Dan accompanied Chris back home.

Tonight Dan had broken the pattern by suggesting they get an ice cream cone in town. One thing hadn't changed, though: Chris's references to Bart.

"You and Bart must've been pretty good friends," Dan said.

"Best friends. He's in fourth grade like me."

Chris had told him that a couple of times already. He also liked to talk about how much of a pain Bart thought his little sister was, although Dan got the impression Chris had a crush on her.

"It must've been tough leaving him behind when you moved," Dan said.

Chris finished off the last of his ice cream cone, saying nothing. Neither had he mentioned the upcoming move. It made Dan wonder if Jill had even mentioned her plans to her brother. They'd seemed tentative at best. If she hadn't shared them with Chris, she might be having second thoughts about leaving. He hoped so. All he could do was wait and see.

"When I was about your age, my friend C.J.'s dad got a job out of state and his family moved away," Dan said. "Worst summer of my life."

"Didn't you have anyone else to play with?"

"I didn't think so at the time," he said. "There were a couple of boys who lived on a farm nearby. Sometimes I'd see them playing, but I never asked if I could join them."

"Were you afraid they'd say no?" Chris asked.

"Absolutely. But when school started, one of those boys sat next to me in class. He and I became really tight. The next summer, I practically lived at that farm."

"There aren't any farms by our house," Chris said. "And anyway, I'm homeschooled."

Thinking back to his own young self, Dan was pretty sure Chris had missed his point deliberately. Like Chris, he'd been undersized, socially awkward and virtually friendless.

Yet the only way he'd reaped the rewards of friendship was by risking rejection. He liked spending time with Chris, but the boy needed to be around other children.

"I'm sure Bart would want you to make new friends." He nodded toward the boys playing tag in the field. "I bet they'd let you play."

Chris shook his head. "They'd beat me up if Bart wasn't with me."

"Nobody's going to beat you up," Dan said. "You're a likable kid."

Chris bowed his head. "Arianne says I'm a nerd, and nobody likes a nerd."

"Who's Arianne?"

Chris continued to gaze down at his feet. "Nobody."

Dan understood the boy's reluctance to tell him about the girl. She sounded like a bully.

"Well, Arianne's wrong," Dan said, "because I like you a lot."

Chris's head rose. "Really?"

"Really." Dan hopped down from the picnic table. "Ready to go?"

Shouts of laughter erupted from the field. "I caught

you!" a boy wearing a red T-shirt yelled in a high-pitched voice. "Now you're it."

Chris looked longingly at the boys, then slowly got down from the picnic table. "Yeah, I'm ready."

The boy obviously wasn't ready to risk rejection in an attempt to make friends. It might be years before he felt comfortable doing that, if ever.

What he needed was some help, and Dan had a great idea that would give him a subtle shove in the right direction.

All he needed was Jill's permission.

THE DOGS WERE BARKING again, the same way they had the other times Jill had swung by Dan's house to pick up Chris.

She didn't let on that the animals unnerved her, even though the rain that had begun to fall made it necessary for her to step inside. She ignored the hundred or so pounds of dog flesh vying for her attention and launched into her spiel.

"I'm sorry I didn't get here sooner," she said. "I stayed late to help Frank—he's Annie's dad—with paperwork. Then he insisted I have a kielbasa sandwich, which was delicious, by the way. And then, would you believe it, I had a flat tire Frank helped me change."

"Hi, Jill." Dan looked the opposite of annoyed, with a lazy smile on his lips that reached his eyes. He even looked good with a five-o'clock shadow and wearing a plain gray T-shirt.

"Hey, Dan." She slowed herself down and returned his smile, genuinely glad to see him. "Is Chris ready to go?"

"You must not have gotten the message I left on

your cell," he said. "I just got back from walking him home."

This marked the first time they'd been alone since the kayaking "lesson." Fine with her. She could handle that. She thought.

"My phone's dead. That's why I didn't call to let you know I'd be late." She backed toward the door. The dogs had stopped barking, which plunged the house into silence broken only by the fall of the rain on the roof. "Sorry to bother you."

"No bother," he said. "I'm actually glad we got our signals crossed. I need to talk to you about Chris."

She stopped backing up and sighed. "He's coming over here too much, isn't he? I told him he didn't have to visit those goats every night."

"No, no. That's not it." He waved a hand. "Come in and sit down. We can discuss it."

She hesitated, then replied, "Okay."

He led her to the family room, dominated by a flat-screen TV mounted on one wall. His sofas, upholstered with a hearty beige fabric, formed a ninety-degree angle around a heavy square sofa table. Some basic floor lamps and a brown leather armchair completed the very masculine decorations.

"Would you like a beer?" he called from the kitchen, which was an extension of the family room.

"Nothing for me," she said. "But you go ahead."

She sat down on one of the sofas and was immediately flanked by his two dogs. They sat perfectly still, not crowding her or clamoring for attention. She tentatively stuck out a hand and stroked the first dog, then the second. Both of them practically moaned in pleasure.

"How'd you get to be so good with dogs?" Dan entered the room, holding a beer bottle.

"I'm not," she said. "We moved a lot when I was growing up, so we never had pets. My mama said it wouldn't be fair to them."

"Could have fooled me." He sat on the sofa catty-corner from her, stretching his long jean-clad legs in front of him. "You knew just what to do with those two. The way to get them to stop barking is to ignore them until they're quiet."

"Is that what you do?"

He laughed. "It's what I should do. I'm excited to see Starsky and Hutch when I get home from work, too, so I don't follow my own advice."

Why that was endearing, Jill couldn't say.

"Starsky and Hutch?" she asked. "Wasn't that a movie?"

"And before that, a television show from the seventies," he said. "I liked the movie so much a friend bought me the first season on DVD. Now I've got quite the collection of TV cop shows."

Probably because he had a highly developed sense of justice, which could turn out to be a negative if his definition of right and wrong didn't coincide with hers.

"So what has Chris done that you want to talk to me about?" she asked.

"It's more what he hasn't done," Dan said. "It doesn't seem like he's made any friends his own age since he moved here."

"He hasn't," Jill said sadly. "But then, he's never had many friends."

"Yea, but it seems like Bart used to be enough for him."

"Bart?" She almost groaned. "He told you about Bart?"

"He talks about him all the time. About Bart's sister, too. I think it was really hard on him to leave them."

Jill rubbed the bridge of her nose. This wasn't good. She thought her brother had grown out of this particular quirk. "Did he mention Bart's sister by name?"

"Sure." Dan took a swig of beer. "Her name's Lisa."

Jill waited for Dan to make the connection, but he looked at her blankly. "Bart and Lisa *Simpson,*" she clarified.

He frowned, then set down his beer on the coffee table. "The cartoon family?"

"You got it." She blew out a breath. "I don't like him to watch the show, but I'm pretty sure he does when I'm not home. Do you know who Milhouse is?"

"Isn't he Bart's best friend?"

"Bart's *intelligent, nerdy* best friend," she clarified. "Milhouse isn't popular with anyone except, well, Bart. I'm afraid Chris identifies with him."

"Wow," Dan said. "Why didn't I figure that out?"

"Maybe you haven't noticed Chris has a problem with lying," she said. "With him spending so much time over here, I should have mentioned it."

"I know he lied to Lindsey about Tinkerbell," Dan said, "but I didn't know it was a problem."

She'd sat her brother down and expressed her disappointment after the Lindsey incident. As always, though, she was faced with an impossible dilemma. How could she get the point across that lying was wrong when they were living a lie?

She had a nearly overwhelming urge to ask Dan for advice. Her gut told her she could trust him. Her brain warned that her gut had been wrong before.

She'd been sure Ray Williams would accept her fervent belief that her brother, a proven liar, was telling the truth about Arianne. Instead Ray had insisted he'd go straight to her father unless she changed her mind about absconding with Chris, forcing her to put the plan into motion early.

If she couldn't trust Ray, whom she'd been dating for three months, how could she trust Dan, a man she'd known for a third of that time and who'd just professed a love for cop shows?

"Chris lies about a lot of things," she said. "It started after his mother died. She was one of those women who made her child the center of the universe. Always taking him somewhere, throwing him parties, showering him with presents and love."

"It must have been heartbreaking for him to lose her," Dan said.

"It was," Jill agreed. "Chris had just started second grade. Our father worked all the time, so after his wife died he hired babysitters and put Chris in after-school care."

"Weren't you living with them?"

"Oh, no," she said. "Growing up I lived with my mama and then I got my own apartment. I saw Chris whenever I could, but my place was about thirty minutes away and I was working a lot of hours myself."

"Bartending?"

"No. I managed a bicycle shop that didn't close until nine at night. Whenever I saw Chris, he'd tell these wild stories. Like about a monkey who played with him at recess. Or the bus driver who let him take the wheel."

"Sounds like he was trying to get attention."

"That's what the school psychologist told my dad," she said. "She said we shouldn't let him get away with the lies, but at the same time we needed to show him how much we loved him."

"Did that work?"

"For a while." Until her father got remarried and unwittingly introduced a whole new problem into Chris's life. Try as she might, Jill had never been able to convince her father that he'd married a bad person.

"Poor kid," Dan said. "It must have been doubly hard on him when your father died."

Jill's heart clutched. Dan was such a good listener that she'd let down her guard. She'd even told him the truth about her last job! If he hadn't mentioned her very-much-alive father, she might have blabbed even more.

"Yeah," she said. "It was."

"Is that when he started talking about Bart Simpson as though he were a real boy?"

"It was around then," Jill said, although Chris had become imaginary friends with Bart soon after she'd spirited him away from Atlanta.

"Is Arianne a cartoon character, too?"

It felt as though someone had cut off Jill's oxygen supply. She forced herself to breathe, to think and most of all not to react. "What do you know about Arianne?"

"I know she told Chris he was a loser," Dan said.

She tried to hide her anxiety. "What else did Chris say about her?"

"That's it. I take it she's a real girl, then?"

Girl? Dan thought Arianne was a girl? Although why

wouldn't he? Adult women who disparaged and scared children were a rare breed, thankfully.

"Chris is too quick to listen to the negatives," she said. "I've been trying to build up his self-confidence."

"Friends his own age would help," Dan said.

"Don't I know it." Jill had lain awake nights thinking about that very thing.

"Have you thought about sending him to Indigo Springs Elementary instead of homeschooling him?"

"He's not ready for that yet." Jill felt bad about misleading Dan regarding her true reasons, but it couldn't be helped. "I signed him up for youth soccer last fall. He lasted one practice. Same thing with Boy Scouts. One meeting. Unfortunately he's not the type of kid who makes friends easily."

"He might if the other kids shared his interests." Dan sat forward on the sofa, his forearms resting on his knees. "Have you thought about getting him involved in 4-H?"

"Can't say that I have." Jill had a fuzzy notion of what the organization stood for. "What is 4-H exactly?"

"It's a youth organization sponsored by the department of agriculture. They do lots of things. Cooking, arts and crafts, horticulture. But the group here in Indigo Springs puts emphasis on working with animals. It's right up Chris's alley."

"That sounds wonderful," Jill said.

"There's more. My boss runs the program. Hope you don't mind, but I took the liberty of mentioning this to Stanley. They have meetings twice a month starting in September and running through May."

Some of Jill's enthusiasm waned. She couldn't promise that she and Chris would even be in Indigo Springs come September. "It figures they wouldn't be active in the summer."

"I didn't say that." Dan's blue eyes shone. "Most of the members of the group are going to Hersheypark this coming Sunday. Stanley said Chris is welcome to come along."

Hersheypark was an amusement park located ninety minutes away in a town Jill had always wanted to visit. She'd heard the streetlights were shaped like Hershey kisses and that the place smelled like the chocolate plant that lent the town its name.

"I don't know about that," she said slowly. "Chris isn't the most daring kid around. I can't imagine he'd ride any of the roller coasters."

"One of the reasons Stanley picked Hersheypark is it includes admission to an adjacent zoo," Dan said. "Chris would like that."

"Probably," Jill said, "but you know how shy he can be. He might be miserable on a trip with a bunch of strangers."

"Then you and I can go with him," Dan said. "Counting Stanley, that'll be three people he knows."

"Three adults," she clarified.

"Three adults who can encourage him to get to know the other kids," Dan said. "What do you say? Can you get the day off?"

Although Jill was scheduled to guide a white water trip on Sunday, finding a substitute on a weekend was usually not a problem. If she couldn't get the entire night off from the Blue Haven, Chuck Dudza almost certainly wouldn't have a problem with her arriving a little late.

"I'm pretty sure I can," she said.

"Great!" Dan said. "It's a date."

A date? What had Jill done? In her eagerness to ease things over for her brother, had she agreed to spend the day with a man she should avoid?

She should backtrack. She should tell him she doubted she'd be able to take the time off work after all. She should...

"Together we'll make sure your brother has a good time." He grinned at her, and she felt stupid. And ungrateful.

Since they'd gone kayaking, Dan hadn't done a single thing to make her think he didn't respect her wishes.

Why, they were alone in his house and he was talking about her brother.

She stood up.

"It sounds like the rain is letting up," she said. "I should get going before it starts up again."

"Okay," he said. No argument. Just okay.

Her imagination was really running away with her.

Dan was proving repeatedly that he was a nice guy. As long as she was careful not to reveal too much about herself or her past, there was no reason they couldn't be friends.

THE WOODEN TRACK ROSE from the ground at Hersheypark, its crazy curves and plunges making it hard to figure out the path of the roller coaster train that was navigating its insane twists.

"Ready to ride the Wildcat, Chris?" Dan asked. With his Ohio State cap slung low over his eyes, dark shorts that ended a few inches shy of his knees and a distressed-graphic T-shirt screen-printed with the image of an eagle, he looked young and vigorous.

"No. Nuh-uh. No way." Chris had barely strayed from Jill's side since they'd boarded the charter bus that morning in Indigo Springs, first sitting next to her, then keeping within a few feet of her at the amusement park's zoo. Now he edged even closer.

The rest of the dozen or so children in their group, who ranged in age from ten to twelve, hurried to get in line, laughing and pointing at the impressive wooden structure. Stanley Kownacki and the three other chaperones followed, not as quickly but just as eagerly.

Stanley had talked up the Wildcat on the bus ride, claiming it reached speeds of up to forty-five miles per hour and was the most thrilling of the park's eleven coasters. Since most of the children didn't meet the minimum height requirements for three of the coasters, Jill thought he'd tailored his comments for the audience.

Still, the Wildcat looked impressively daunting. Chris certainly seemed to think so.

"Are you sure you don't want to try it, honey?" Jill wished she had the magic words to help her brother conquer his fear. "It might be fun."

Chris stared down at the ground, saying nothing.

Jill shot Dan a resigned look. That morning while they'd visited mountain lions, black bears and gray wolves in the eleven-acre walk-through zoo, she'd quietly reiterated her concerns that Chris would be too timid to try many of the rides.

"He might surprise you," Dan had said.

She'd wanted to believe that. Unfortunately, she doubted Chris was about to spring any bombshells on her.

"Jill, have you seen Brittany Waverly?" Dan asked, a non sequitur if she'd ever heard one.

Brittany was the only girl on the trip and the sole child besides Chris who wasn't a 4-H member. Brittany's mother, one of the chaperones, had brought her along, to the obvious horror of her older brother Timmy.

Jill indicated the line, where the adorable young girl was craning her neck and bouncing on her toes while the boys ignored her. She was maybe nine, but at about four foot three or four she was almost the same height as Chris. If the two of them were any shorter, they wouldn't meet the minimum height requirements for the ride. "She's over there with the rest of the kids."

Almost as if she knew they were talking about her, Brittany looked over at them. Jill noticed Dan give the girl a slight nod. Brittany immediately broke off from the group, skipping across the pavement on her pink tennis shoes, her blond ponytails flying.

"C'mon, Chris." Her high-pitched, little-girl voice sounded breathless. "I saved you a place in line."

Chris shook his head.

Brittany glanced at Dan, who gave her another of those puzzling nods. "I used to be scared, too," Brittany said. "Then I—"

"I'm not scared of some dumb old roller coaster!" Chris denied hotly.

"Then c'mon!" Brittany was fairly dancing in place. "We're going to lose our place!"

She pivoted on one of her dainty feet and dashed away. Chris hesitated for a second, then ran after her. Brittany turned, smiling and backpedaling while he caught up to her.

"I bet you scream," she said.

Jill couldn't hear her brother's answer. Chris's vigorous head shake, however, spoke volumes. So did Dan's wide grin.

She narrowed her eyes. "What is going on, Dan?"

"Your brother just agreed to ride the roller coaster." Smugness practically oozed from him.

"No. I meant what's going on with you and that sweet little Brittany? I swear, it looked like you were egging her on."

"You noticed that, huh?" He seemed proud of himself. "Once she remembered what she was supposed to say, she was a good little actress. I'd say she earned her five bucks."

"Why, Dan Maguire." Jill balanced one hand on her hip while the full extent of his plan struck her. "Are you saying you paid for a child to embarrass Chris into riding the roller coaster?"

"Yep," he said, totally without shame.

Jill let the laugh she'd been holding back break forth. "How did you know it would work?"

"It's called peer pressure," he answered. "I have three sisters. They didn't get paid a cent and the same thing worked on me when I was a kid."

He related the story without a trace of self-consciousness, painting a picture of a childhood that sounded exceedingly ordinary. How she wished she could provide a fraction of that sort of normalcy for Chris. Maybe, with a little bit of help, she could.

"You are a man of hidden talents," she remarked.

He waggled his eyebrows with comic exaggeration. "Say the word and I'll show you more of my talents."

She swatted at his arm, laughing. "Now you're being silly."

"Maybe and maybe not." He slung an arm around her shoulders. Her pulse jumped and her senses flared. She stayed put, though. Here at an amusement park in the middle of the afternoon, she was well equipped to withstand her involuntary physical reactions to him. "I can promise you this. I won't try anything on the roller coaster. Even I'm not that talented."

He started walking her in the direction of the ride. She craned her neck to look up at him. It wasn't fair, but the man was even good-looking from this angle. "I don't remember saying I'd go on the Wildcat with you."

"What are you? Scared?" His eyes danced.

"Bring it on, mister!" she said. "But don't you dare tell me not to scream. That's part of the fun."

"Wouldn't dream of it." He winked. "You can grab my knee if you want, though."

"You wish," she said.

"That's right," he said good-naturedly. "I do."

As it turned out, she grabbed the handlebars. They were too far back in line to take the same coaster train as the rest of their group. Somehow they wound up in the last car, which seemed to fly off the tracks at every wild turn and stomach-plunging dip.

Jill was breathless and laughing when they exited

the ride. Chris ran up to them, his thin chest puffed up. "Did you see me! I didn't even scream!"

"Of course you didn't." Dan clapped the boy on his shoulder. "Your sister, on the other hand, sounded like a fire alarm."

"Roller coasters scare girls," Chris said knowingly. "Brittany screamed, too."

"Hey! Like I told Dan, screaming's part of the fun. There's no shame in it," Jill said. "Half the guys on our coaster were shrieking. Why, I even think I heard a yowl from—"

"Shhh." Dan placed two fingers over her lips before she could fill in his name. "I can't let you ruin my macho image."

The ability to speak momentarily left her, but she did manage to roll her eyes.

Chris wasn't listening, anyway. He was halfway between them and the other children. Brittany was the only one paying attention to him.

"We're going on the Lightning Racers next!" she called, then skipped along with the large group of boys.

Chris followed, but at a distance. Small steps, Jill told herself. She counted it as a triumph that he was no longer plastered to her side.

"The Lightning Racers are dueling roller coasters," Dan explained. "You race to see who finishes first."

Both the Wildcat and the Lightning Racers were in a section of the park known as the midway. They hurried to keep up with the children, walking past a Ferris wheel and a steel coaster called the Wild Mouse. Dan explained that the allure of the Wild Mouse was the illusion the four-passenger car would fall off the track.

"How do you know so much about the coasters here?" she asked. "Have you been to this park before?"

"Nope, but Stanley has. He's a roller-coaster nut. He's been talking about this trip for weeks. Notice we didn't visit the chocolate factory. Not Stanley's priority."

The older vet was indeed leading the group, sort of resembling an aging Pied Piper in baggy madras shorts and a T-shirt. Once they reached the surprisingly short line at the Lightning Racers, Stanley organized their group into teams. He instructed half of them to ride the Lightning Red coaster and half the Thunder Green.

Jill and Dan wound up in a middle car of the red coaster. Chris, again paired with Brittany, settled in directly across from them in the green coaster.

"Thunder rules!"

"Lightning's faster!"

"You're going down!"

The 4-H'ers shouted rallying cries as the coasters sat idle on the track. Jill noticed that Chris, although silent, was smiling.

"Get ready to eat our wind!" Dan yelled just as the coasters took off.

"Good one!" Jill told him before the wind in her face robbed her of speech.

The coasters raced around the side-by-side tracks, affording glimpses of the riders in the other cars between plunges and hairpin turns.

Jill let her screams rip. At the end of the ride, when the green racer won by the narrowest of margins, she was surprised to find herself clutching Dan's arm, her face buried in his shoulder.

She let go of him. "Sorry."

"That's okay." His teeth flashed. "You're cute when you're afraid."

Stanley and the 4-H'ers didn't hesitate when they got off the ride, circling back around and getting in line again. Jill and Dan followed the group, walking alongside two of the other chaperones, both mothers wearing fanny packs and sensible sneakers.

"I could use something to drink," Jill remarked through a suddenly parched throat.

"Go ahead and take a break." Liz Waverly, Brittany's mother, made the offer. "Chris is your brother, right? I'll keep an eye on him. You can catch up to us later."

"Why, thanks," Jill said. "Are you sure it's not too much trouble?"

"Absolutely sure," Liz said, "so go enjoy each other when you have the chance."

"Enjoy each other?" Jill repeated a moment later. They were headed for a slushie stand they'd passed when they'd first arrived on their mad dash to the Wildcat. "That was a strange choice of words."

"Not really," Dan said. "Liz probably thinks we're a couple."

Jill was afraid of that. "We should tell her we're just friends."

"So I won you over, did I?" He slung an arm around her shoulders. She willed herself to breathe and not to read too much into the friendly gesture. "I remember when you said it wouldn't be smart for us to be friends.

You said Penelope would never accept that was all there was between us."

Judging by the warmth rapidly spreading through her body, it still wasn't smart. These past few weeks, though, she'd discovered that some things were worth the risk.

A friendship with Dan was one of them.

"No way am I admitting you won me over," she said. "I don't want you getting a big head."

He threw his very nicely proportioned head back and laughed.

The day passed quickly, with the children clamoring to stay until the park closed at ten o'clock. Stanley gave in—not that it took much persuading.

By the time the bus was thirty minutes into the trip back to Indigo Springs, most of the children and some of the adult chaperones were asleep.

"Even Gigantor looks tired," Jill whispered to Dan from her seat next to him in the back of the bus. Across the aisle the enormous stuffed teddy bear he'd won on the midway had a seat to himself.

"Gigantor had it easy," Dan said. "I carried him all over the park."

"Thanks again for winning him for me," Jill said.

"Don't mention it," he said. "I knew if I threw enough darts, odds were some of them would hit a balloon."

"You spent more money to win that bear than it would have cost to buy a new one."

"Probably," he said, "but it gave me the opportunity to impress you with my mad dart-throwing skills."

She giggled, then leaned her head against the seat and turned. She liked the way the ends of his black hair curled and the way his long, straight nose, strong chin and full mouth looked in profile. "Just in case you haven't realized it, I had a wonderful day. Thank you."

"I didn't do much," he said.

"You arranged for Chris and me to go on this trip. If not for you, my little brother might have grown into an old man who'd never ridden a roller coaster."

He smiled lazily. This late in the day, his skin showed the barest hint of stubble, somehow making him even better looking. "If not for Brittany, you mean."

She nodded to indicate a seat three rows in front of them where Chris and Brittany sat side by side. After going on the Wildcat together, they'd partnered up on every ride.

Judging by the slightly slumped position of Chris's body, he appeared to be asleep. Even awake, he didn't have much to say to Brittany. Most likely they'd gravitated to each other because none of the other children showed any interest in riding with them.

"I'm glad Chris had Brittany to hang out with today," Jill said. "I can't see them becoming close friends, though."

"Me, either," Dan said. "But it's a start. Come fall, Chris might be more open to joining 4-H."

"We can only hope," Jill said, hearing the wistful note in her voice.

"That sounds like you've changed your mind about moving."

She hadn't thought about relocating at all recently. After more than a year in hiding, she'd concluded she couldn't spend every minute looking over her shoulder.

Today she hadn't once considered somebody at the amusement park might be tailing her and Chris. Neither, however, could she pretend she was free to lead a normal life.

"The move's still in the cards, but it's on hold." She changed the subject before he could comment. "Is everyone on this bus asleep except us?"

"I hear some murmuring in the front of the bus," he said, "and I'm pretty sure the bus driver's awake."

She smiled. "I'm sort of sleepy, too."

"You work too much." He smoothed a lock of her hair back from her face. A shiver danced through her. "It can't be good for you to burn the candle at both ends."

"Thanks, Dad," she teased, partly to hide how good it felt to have someone worry about her for a change.

Now that she'd admitted to her fatigue, she had a hard time keeping her eyes open. Her head lolled. She straightened it.

"Go ahead," he invited. "Lean on me."

Probably all sorts of reasons existed why she shouldn't accept his offer. She admitted she was too tired to figure out what they were. Sighing, she surrendered to temptation and rested her head against his shoulder. Immediately she was enveloped by his scent and a sense of peace.

She snuggled against him and closed her eyes. She imagined she felt a kiss against her hair but she could have been dreaming, so quickly did she sink into sleep.

CHAPTER EIGHT

"YOU'RE COMING BY the house tonight to see Tinkerbell and Bluebell, right?" Dan walked through the back corridors of the vet's office with Chris Jacobi. It was nearly six o'clock, closing time.

The boy shook his head, which came as a surprise. Chris had begun volunteering at the office once a week, but religiously visited the goats twice daily.

"Mrs. Feldman is having some dumb old card game tonight," Chris said. "Jill is making me go out for pizza with Lindsey and her mom and dad."

That explained the message Jill had left for Dan earlier today that the Whitmores would pick up Chris.

"That sounds awful!" Dan ruffled the boy's soft, curly hair. "I can't believe you have to eat pizza!"

Chris seemed confused. "You don't like pizza?"

"It was a joke, buddy." The young boy was entirely too serious. "Of course I like pizza. Why don't you want to go?"

He thrust out his lower lip. "I want to see Tinkerbell and Bluebell."

"You see them every night."

"They like me."

"Lindsey and her parents like you, too," Dan said just as they reached the waiting area. Lindsey was the only occupant. She jumped to her feet, looking young and breezy in a pale blue sundress. A smile wreathed her pretty face.

"Hi, Dr. Maguire," she said, and he returned the greeting. She switched her attention to Chris. "Ready to go, Chris? My mom and dad are saving a table. The place is already packed."

"Be sure to eat an extra piece for me," Dan said.

Despite the grousing he'd done to Dan, Chris followed Lindsey obediently. The door opened before they reached it, admitting a familiar tall, gray-haired gentleman wearing a neon-orange shirt.

"Hi, Mayor Bradford." Lindsey beamed at him. "Love the shirt!"

"It is nice, isn't it?" Charlie Bradford looked down at himself and brushed at some imaginary pieces of lint. "Would you believe my wife wants me to get rid of it?"

"I know clothes, and that's a keeper," Lindsey said, her grin growing.

"My sentiments exactly!" Charlie said.

"See you, Mayor." Lindsey moved past him, with Chris silently trailing.

"I can't get used to being called that," Charlie told Dan as he walked deeper into the office, shaking his head. "I never counted on becoming a politician."

"You're a good one," Dan said, then grinned. "Or so Stanley is fond of telling me."

Charlie laughed. "I got that old coot fooled. Is he done cleaning Sweet Thing's teeth yet?"

Sweet Thing was Charlie and Teresa Bradford's dog, who made up in temperament what she lacked in looks.

Part pug and part something unidentifiable, the much-loved dog proved that beauty was overrated.

"Just finished," Dan said.

"I'll go on back, then." Charlie headed toward the exam rooms, then hesitated. "Hey, wasn't that Jill Jacobi's little brother with Lindsey?"

"Yeah," Dan said. "He's been helping around the office. Cleaning the cages, sweeping the floor, that kind of stuff."

"You don't say." Charlie stroked his chin. "How well do you know his sister?"

Not nearly as well as he'd like to, Dan thought.

"Jill and I are friends," Dan said.

"Friends?" Stanley interjected. Dan hadn't heard the other vet come up behind him. He was cradling Sweet Thing in his arms, his face more pinched than the dog's. "You didn't give me the impression friendship was what you were after. You change your mind or what?"

He hadn't. With each passing day, he became more sure of his feelings for Jill. He just hadn't expected anyone to ask him to explain himself.

"Give the kid time, Stanley," Charlie interjected, coming forward and taking his dog from his friend's arms. "There's a lot to be said for relationships that begin as friendships. That's how Teresa and I started out."

"Thank you, Charlie," Dan said.

"Don't mention it," he said, "especially since I'm about to ask for a favor. Have you heard of the Poconos Challenge?"

When Dan shook his head, the mayor explained it

was an inaugural mountain bike race that would take place in the fall.

"There will be overnight stops in selected Pocono towns," Charlie said. "It'll be great for tourism. That's why I want Indigo Springs to be one of the stops."

"I don't see how I can help you," Dan said.

"Oh. I see what's coming," Stanley said. "Charlie's office has been working up a proposal and he's trying to talk your *friend* into submitting it."

"We'll have the best chance of success if a mountain biker presents the proposal, not to mention helps with the route options. Jill's the logical choice," Charlie said. "I've been working on her for two or three weeks with no luck. Now you, on the other hand, she might find harder to resist."

"I'm not so sure about that." Dan thought she'd been doing a pretty good job of remaining immune to his supposed charm.

"It's worth a shot," Charlie said. "Stanley and I are going over to the Blue Haven tonight so I can have another go at her. We'd love to have you join us."

"Even if I believe that Jill should be allowed to make up her own mind about submitting the proposal?" Dan asked.

"That's the thing," Charlie said. "She had a blast working on the spring festival. She told me to come to her if I needed help on anything else. It beats me why she keeps saying no. So what do you say?"

Dan hesitated. Given Jill's passion for mountain biking and the fact that she used to manage a bicycle shop, it did seem odd that she hadn't embraced the assignment.

"Come on," Charlie pleaded. "I'm the mayor. I'm supposed to have heightened powers of persuasion. It'll look bad if I can't even talk a guy into coming to a bar."

Dan laughed, figuring it couldn't hurt to add his vote of confidence that Jill could handle the job. Besides, the more time he spent around her, the better his chances of wearing her down.

"Okay," he said. "I'm in."

THE RAUCOUS STRAINS of "Ain't Nothin' but a Hound Dog" filled the Blue Haven, alerting Annie that Buster Dreher was at the controls of the jukebox.

Buster danced across the floor, gyrating his hips and torso. His pants were too tight for a slightly overweight man in his early fifties. He wore his jet-black hair slicked back from his face. A lock fell onto his forehead from his otherwise perfect pompadour.

"Elvis is in the house," Buster shouted, then threw back his head and laughed.

It might have been funny if Jill hadn't watched Buster perform the same act at least once a week for the past year. So, apparently, had everyone else. She spotted only one person in the bar who was laughing with Buster.

Then again, she would have noticed her friend Dan no matter what he was doing.

Since he'd come into the Blue Haven with Stanley and Charlie Bradford, the person in the house she'd been most interested in wasn't fake Elvis.

The three men were sharing a pitcher of beer, the same way Stanley and Charlie did every week. But why had the two longtime pals broken from tradition and invited Dan along? And why hadn't Dan told her he'd be here tonight?

"Did you forget about my whiskey on the rocks?" called a man sitting at the bar. She whirled to face the guy, a tourist who'd been insistent about his preferred brand.

"Course not. I wouldn't do a thing like that," she said. "It's coming right up."

She plucked a glass from an overhead shelf, set it down on the bar, filled it with ice cubes and poured. Despite a mental reminder to focus on her work, her gaze returned to Dan. He was really quite a good-looking man. He had a strong profile, his nose long and straight, his chin square, the dark hair springing back from a high forehead.

Almost as though he felt her looking at him, he turned his head and met her eyes across the room. His lips curved into a smile, warm and slow. And…flirtatious? No. That couldn't be. The two of them were friends.

"Hey, lady, you trying to get me drunk or what?" The tourist's voice once again broke her out of a trance.

She dragged her gaze from Dan, and the tourist pointed at the glass, which she'd filled nearly to the brim with whiskey. She abruptly tilted the bottle upright before the amber liquid spilled over.

"Sorry about that," she said.

"Nothing to apologize for," he retorted, rising from his stool and sliding the glass toward him. He lowered his head and sipped the first inch before picking up the drink.

She made a mental note to pay more attention to the tourist's sobriety level and less to Dan.

"Hey there, good-looking." Dan sauntered up to the bar, wreaking havoc with her plan. He wore a blue oxford cloth shirt with the sleeves rolled up, which showed off the definition in his arms and called attention to the color of his eyes. They were smiling. "Having a good night?"

"I always do." She felt a surge of joy, which wasn't unexpected. She was generally a happy person. "I'm surprised to see you here."

He leaned forward, resting his forearms on the bar, and indicated with a slight nod that she should come nearer. She did, leaning so close she could see the beginnings of his five-o'clock shadow. She had a wild urge to run her hand over his lower face.

"I was roped into it," he whispered, those blue eyes trained on her. "The mayor thinks I can persuade you to come over to our table on your break. He has something he wants to talk to you about."

Oh, no. Not this again. She straightened, the crazy spell broken, and crossed her arms over her chest. "The bike race?"

"How'd you guess?"

"Charlie does not do subtle," she said. "That darned man has been trying to get me to help him out with that for weeks."

"He doesn't understand why you won't say yes," Dan said. "He seems to think you're into community work."

That was her fault for gushing about how much she'd enjoyed working on the spring festival. But how was she to know the next opportunity to help out would involve a mountain bike race?

"It's in Charlie's best interest to believe all his citizens enjoy community work." Jill kept her reply carefully neutral. "He's a wily old devil."

"You got that right. How do you think he convinced me to help him persuade you?" Dan winked at her. "Don't worry. I'm taking your side, whatever it is."

The problem was that she couldn't adequately explain why it was imperative she refuse, Jill ruminated a short time later when she joined the three men.

"Hi, Jill." Charlie greeted her like an old friend. "We were just talking about Chase and Kelly. Did you hear they went off to Vegas last week and got married?"

The unexpected subject momentarily threw her. Chase, the mayor's only child, had been living with his fiancée for nearly a year. They were in the process of adopting an adorable two-year-old named Toby who was much better off with Chase than with his biological mother, a con artist serving a prison term.

"I heard." She took the chair Dan held out for her. Their bodies brushed, the touch electric. She stole a look at him, and he was smiling. "It's all over town by now."

"Hell of a thing," Charlie said. "They wait all this time, then run off like that. Who does that?"

"That's what you and Teresa did," Stanley said. "Chase told me he got the idea from you."

"He should know better than to use his old man as an example." Charlie shook his graying head. "They say they didn't want anyone to make a fuss, but a fuss is what they're getting. Teresa sent you all an invitation to the party we're having for them on Sunday night, right?"

"I'll be sorry to miss it," Stanley said. "I'm going out of town on a fishing trip."

"I'll be there," Jill said.

"How about you, Dan?" Charlie asked.

"I'm coming," he said.

"Really?" Jill peered at him. "You know Kelly and Chase?"

"I know Chase." Dan shifted in his seat, bringing his body closer to her. His clean scent overrode the smell of beer. "He's a wildlife conservation officer. Where do you think he brings the injured animals he comes across?"

She hadn't thought of that. With Buster singing another Elvis song in the background and Dan only inches from her, it was hard to think at all.

"As much as I love talking about my son, Jill will have to get back to work soon." Charlie leaned forward, his full attention zeroed in on her. "So let's talk about the bike race."

She shifted so she was a little farther from Dan, the better to keep her wits about her.

"Tell me," Charlie continued, "did I get it wrong about how much fun you had working on the spring festival?"

"You're not wrong," she said, "but you already have people working on this far more qualified than I am."

"None of them is a cyclist," he said, "and that's what I think would put us over the top. All you'd need to do is figure out a couple of route options that would end on Main Street and meet with the nominating committee in Lake Wallenpaupack to present the proposal."

"Shouldn't you have somebody on the borough council

do that?" Jill wouldn't let on that she'd been meaning to visit the Poconos Mountain community, having heard it was almost as pretty as Indigo Springs.

"Not necessarily," Charlie said. "But speaking of the council, I think Chad's right. You should run for office."

"I'd vote for you." Stanley set his beer mug down with a thump while she mentally damned the quiet pharmacist for opening his mouth. "How about you, Dan?"

"I'd *campaign* for her," he said, "except Jill might have reasons for not going into politics."

She drew in a quick breath, nonsensically afraid he'd read her mind. Then reason surfaced. She'd told him she was thinking about moving and asked that he keep her confidence. He was on her side, exactly as he'd claimed.

"How did we get on this tangent?" Jill asked. "I never once thought about being a council member before Chad brought it up."

"You're right. Running for council is a big decision," Charlie said, as though she were actually considering it. "Tell you what. I won't pressure you about the council if you agree to submit the proposal."

She chewed her bottom lip. The risk of running into someone she knew in the biking world was slight, given that they weren't in Georgia. A greater hazard was drawing suspicion to herself by continuing to refuse a reasonable request, one that everybody could see she wanted to accept.

"When is the proposal due?" she asked.

Charlie grinned. "The weekend after next."

"Okay," Jill said, "but you can't blame me if we don't

get the nod. I'm not good at talking people into doing things."

"With that sweet smile and that Southern accent of yours, I've got to disagree with that," Dan said. "You could talk me into just about anything."

A shiver of pleasure danced over her, more worrisome than the prospect of reentering the mountain bike community.

She hadn't imagined it.

Just when she'd started to let down her guard around Dan, he'd started flirting with her.

And she wasn't at all sure she could handle it.

CHAPTER NINE

DAN COULDN'T HAVE TIMED his arrival better.

As soon as he stepped onto the curb in front of Teresa and Charlie Bradford's house Sunday night, he spotted Jill approaching on the sidewalk a half block away. She carried a silver gift bag topped with an elaborate matching bow.

He pocketed the keys to his pickup and headed for her, noticing it was taking him twice as long to close the gap as it should have.

Because, he realized, she was frozen in place.

"Is it my imagination," he asked as he approached her, "or are you not moving?"

"I figured you might not see me if I didn't move," she said with a lift of her shoulders, "but I must've miscalculated."

"Just a little." He felt the corners of his mouth rise. She was wearing another of her funky outfits—a yellow minidress with a belt slung low across her hips, multicolored beads draped over her neck, matching bracelets on her arms. "You shouldn't have worn that if you didn't want to be noticed."

She looked down at herself. "Good point."

"So why are you trying to be invisible?"

"The same reason I told you not to pick me up. People

already think we're dating without us fueling the fire by arriving together."

He didn't consider that prospect to be a negative. He'd take all the help he could get in his quest to change her mind about dating him.

"The party's already in full swing." He lightly placed a hand at her back. Her body jumped slightly but perceptibly. Yep. He was right. She did react every time he touched her. "Nobody's going to pay us much notice."

"Famous last words," she muttered, but went along. When they reached the door, he punched the bell with his index finger, then bent his head close to hers. He deliberately took her hand, this time noticing a slight tremor. He was encouraged that she didn't yank it away.

"By the way," he said, his breath brushing her ear, "you look especially lovely in yellow."

She met his eyes, her mouth parting but no words emerging. With her glossy black hair, green eyes and freckles, she was becoming the standard by which he measured all other women. Lately all he could think about was how much he wanted to kiss her. Her mouth was close. So close.

The door abruptly swung open, breaking the spell. Instead of one of the Bradfords, it was Penelope Pollock, wearing a white halter dress that showed off the tan she'd acquired during her second honeymoon trip to Hawaii.

"You two make such a cute couple!" she practically squealed.

Annie Whitmore was passing behind Penelope,

holding a drink containing a colorful miniature umbrella. A laugh was on her lips, her husband Ryan's arm around her.

"Look, Annie! Ryan! Didn't I tell you Jill and Dan were dating?" Penelope beamed, her tan making her teeth seem almost blindingly white. "I knew you two were right for each other."

Jill slanted Dan an exasperated look and jerked her hand from his. She didn't, however, deny Penelope's assumption. He'd like to think he was making inroads, but it was just as likely she realized disavowal would be pointless.

Penelope opened the door wide. "Come on in. You're the last ones to arrive."

"Hey, look who's here," Charlie Bradford called, coming forward to take the gift bag from Jill and bottle of wine from Dan. His wife, Teresa, was at his side, looking elegant in a summery pantsuit, her silvery-blond hair swept off her neck. Charlie had dressed for the occasion, too, forsaking the neon-orange he'd worn the other day for more subdued colors. "Teresa, you know Jill."

"Certainly," Teresa said pleasantly. "Jill's the one you browbeat into submitting that proposal for you."

"*Charmed* into submitting, dear." Charlie's eyes crinkled at the corners. "I'm not sure if you know the lucky guy with her. Dan Maguire is the vet who works with Stanley."

"Nice to meet you, Dan." Teresa took one of his hands in both of hers, then included Jill in her gracious smile. "I'm so glad you both could come."

"We're glad to be here," Dan said before Jill could

state they hadn't come together. "Where's the happy couple?"

"Through the house on the deck," Charlie said. "You'll see why Teresa and I bought this place when you get back there. Just call us the entertainers!"

The Bradford house was indeed made for entertaining. A large family room with high ceilings led to a spacious, screened-in deck complete with skylights, a whirring ceiling fan and recessed lighting. White chrysanthemums in gold vases graced tables covered in white lace. Shiny satin ribbons in white and gold had been placed in strategic places. A "Just Married" banner in matching colors hung above the venue.

Chase stood at the center of the deck with the woman who must surely be his bride. Their arms encircled each other's waists while they held champagne glasses in opposite hands. Her dress was red and so was his shirt. That wasn't the only thing that matched. Their wide smiles were nearly identical.

"They look so thrilled to be married," Jill remarked.

The newlyweds, however, were far from the only happy couple present. The place was ripe with them.

There were Sara Brenneman and Michael Donahue. Sara was an attorney who stood out because of her height and the dynamic colors she favored, like the aqua dress she wore tonight. She'd married Michael, a partner in Johnny Pollock's construction business, in a big church wedding earlier that summer.

Sara and Michael were talking to Johnny and a heavily pregnant woman with brown hair even curlier than Jill's. The woman held a glass of what looked like ginger ale. A man of medium height with brown hair that hung to his collar absently rubbed her back.

On the other side of the deck Annie Whitmore was twirling the umbrella in her drink and laughing uproariously at something her husband, Ryan, said. Ryan was the family physician who'd given Dan his last physical.

"I feel like we've stepped into *The Twilight Zone*," Jill said in a voice soft enough that only Dan could hear. "We're the only people here who aren't part of a couple."

"Dan! Jill!" Penelope motioned them over to the kitchen adjacent to the family room, where she was filling a wineglass with ruby liquid. "Would you like me to pour you some wine?"

"Thanks, but I'll take a beer." Dan withdrew a bottle from the cooler in the corner of the kitchen and popped the top.

"I'd love some wine," Jill said. "When did you and Johnny get back from Hawaii, Penelope?"

"Last night. I promise to bore you later with details of our trip, but first I want to know when this happened." Penelope used her index finger to point back and forth from Jill to Dan.

Jill spoke first. "I hate to disappoint you, Penelope, but we didn't come together."

"Johnny and I used to make plans to meet up, too. Sometimes we'd pretend we were strangers just to spice things up. I recommend it." Penelope's eyes lit up and she waved. "Oh, my gosh. Laurie Grieb looks like she's going to have that baby any day. Isn't it cute how Kenny's hovering over her?"

She bustled off in the direction of the expectant couple, who Dan now knew were the Griebs. Soft classical music played in the background, but Dan still heard Jill sigh.

"I'm never going to get through to her that we aren't an item, am I?" Jill asked.

"Highly doubtful."

"Then I guess we might as well go congratulate Chase and Kelly together."

There was nothing he'd like better. "I've never met Kelly."

"You'll like her." Jill gestured to the other woman with her wineglass. "Everybody does. Did you hear how they met?" At Dan's shake of the head, she continued, "It's a wild story. Kelly was falsely accused of kidnapping a baby and jumped bail to clear her name. Her trail led her to Indigo Springs."

"I heard something about that," Dan said. "Didn't Chase help her find the real kidnapper and set things right with the authorities?"

"He did. And now they're married and the parents of a little boy they adore," Jill said. "C'mon. I'll introduce you to Kelly."

The new bride had girl-next-door good looks and a sweetness that emanated from her. She greeted Dan warmly, then turned to Jill. "It's so nice to see you."

"It's nice to see you married." Jill took the other woman's left hand. A white-gold wedding band complemented a diamond engagement ring. "You two are great at keeping a secret."

"We eloped because we didn't want anybody to make a fuss over us." She cut her eyes at her husband. "I know people think getting married in Las Vegas is corny, but it wasn't like that at all. Elvis wasn't anywhere around, and we were in a gazebo covered with these beautiful flowers beside this amazing fountain. It was the most romantic moment of my life."

"Amen to that." Chase looked like his father. He had the same tall, lean build and thick hair, although his was brown instead of gray. "We didn't get the message across to my dad about not making a fuss, though."

"Teresa was actually the one who did the planning," Kelly said, then directed her next comments to Dan. "She and Chase's late mother were best friends. She's loved Chase like he was her own son for a long time."

"She loves Toby like a grandson, too," Chase said.

"Speaking of Toby," Jill said, "thanks for letting Chris be there while Lindsey babysits."

"The more kids who are around, the happier Toby is," Kelly said. "And Chris seems like a very nice boy."

"Lindsey said you bought him some goats, Dan." Chase looked dubious. "Did I hear her right?"

"I only bought him one goat. We found the other," Dan said, then related the entire story.

"You are such a good guy to do that," Kelly exclaimed. "No wonder you won Jill over!"

"We're not—" Jill began.

"Attention, everyone!" Charlie's booming voice drowned out all the other noise on the deck. "It's time to cut the cake."

Teresa held the French doors to the deck open for Charlie as he wheeled in a small table containing a three-tiered cake decorated with alternating layers of chocolate and vanilla frosting.

"It's beautiful!" Kelly cried, eagerly taking the knife Teresa held out to her. Chase put his hand over hers and they both sliced through the bottom layer of the cake.

Charlie launched into an off-key rendition of the song "Sugar, Sugar," his voice cracking on the "honey, honey" line. Soon everyone joined in, most of them humming because they weren't sure of the lyrics.

"We love you guys," Kelly said.

"But we're still glad we eloped." Chase kissed Kelly lingeringly on the lips, then addressed his friends. "No offense, but it was kind of wonderful having my beautiful wife all to myself."

Jill blinked a few times, and Dan realized her eyes were dewy. He took her hand and squeezed it. He noticed some of the people in the room, Penelope most notably, looking at them, smiling and nodding.

Jill was right. She'd never be able to convincingly deny they weren't a couple after tonight.

He couldn't pretend he wasn't happy about that.

KENNY GRIEB STROKED the acoustic guitar, producing an amazingly clear sound as he sang yet another love song. Jill felt as though he'd reached inside her and tugged. From the rapt expressions on the faces of the others gathered around Kenny on the Bradford deck, she wasn't the only one.

"He's amazing," she whispered to Dan.

Kenny had brought out the guitar as a surprise for the newly married couple, singing a truly beautiful arrangement of "Forever and for Always," which had been playing in the chapel when Chase and Kelly got married.

One request had led to another until the hosts and all

of their guests were listening to Kenny put on a show. Jill had heard he'd once been a hard-drinking regular at the Blue Haven. Tonight, however, he'd passed up alcohol entirely in solidarity with his pregnant wife.

"Incredible," Dan agreed.

His chair was next to Jill's, his arm around her shoulders, his fingers playing with the short hairs at her nape. Laurie looked over at them and smiled, her eyes softening. Up to this point Laurie had been one of the only people at the party who'd yet to mistake them for a couple.

Jill could understand the confusion.

Dan had barely left her side. She'd noticed before that he was a toucher. He'd outdone himself tonight, putting his arm around her shoulders, touching her hair, stroking her cheek.

No wonder their friends were getting the wrong idea.

The last strains of the song faded away. There were a few seconds of silence, followed by applause. Laurie put her fingers in the sides of her mouth and whistled.

"Do you know 'Fifty Ways to Leave Your Lover'?" Charlie shouted out.

"May I remind you this is a wedding reception, dear," Teresa told her husband gently.

"Good point," Charlie conceded.

"Kenny needs a break anyway," Laurie said, laughing. "And I need some more of that delicious cake. Everyone knows a pregnant woman can eat as much as she likes."

"Hear, hear!" Johnny Pollock said. "I don't have an excuse, but I want some more, too."

"I call dibs on a chocolate piece," Kenny added.

A small contingent headed for the kitchen. Dan didn't move, his hand lightly caressing Jill's shoulder. "Can I get you another piece of cake?" he asked.

Spoken exactly like a boyfriend.

Enough, she thought, was enough.

"No, thanks," she said. "You can come with me."

She sprang to her feet, heading into the house before any of the other guests could waylay her. Dan was slow to follow, so she doubled back and grabbed his hand.

"Where are we going?" he asked when they reached the family room.

She explored the possibilities. She spied a closed door near the kitchen and opened it, dragging him inside with her. The small room with the tiled floor smelled mountain fresh. A top-loading washing machine and a front-loading dryer hugged one wall. There was barely enough space left over for the two of them.

Dan balanced a hand on the top of the washing machine and smiled down at her. "Now's not the best time to do laundry."

She wasn't going to think about how charmingly one corner of his mouth lifted when he smiled. "We need to talk," she said.

"Here?" He reached out a hand and caressed her cheek.

"Here's perfect." She ignored the shivery sensation where his fingers touched her skin. "I needed to get you somewhere private to tell you to stop touching me."

He grinned. "Usually that works the other way around."

"You're still doing it."

His fingers had moved to her collarbone, absently rubbing over her skin. "What am I doing?"

"Touching me. Nobody will ever believe we're not a couple if you keep that up."

He straightened, tipped her chin so she was looking at him and ran his fingertips over her lips. "Then why are you letting me?"

"Because..." Her voice trailed off. She knew there was a reason. She was just having a hard time coming up with it.

"Don't say it's the wine," he said. "I've been paying attention and you only had one glass all night."

It was all she ever drank. She didn't like not having her wits about her.

"It's not the wine," she said. "It's because I know you don't mean anything by it. You're one of those people who are always touching other people."

"No, I'm not." His gaze locked with hers. "You're the only person I'm always touching."

"Because you and I are friends." Her voice trembled.

"Because I want to be more than your friend," he said.

"But we agreed—"

"I didn't agree to anything," he interrupted, his eyes still on hers. "My feelings haven't changed. I want to see where this attraction we have for each other leads."

Denying she was attracted to him would be fruitless. Even if she hadn't already admitted as much, he might be able to tell that goose bumps had popped up on her skin where he'd touched her.

"We've already been over this," she said in a soft, weak voice. "I'm not staying in Indigo Springs."

"The more I think about that, the less I view it as a problem," Dan said. "I'm not looking for anything long-term. An uncomplicated relationship would suit me just fine."

"But not me!"

"Why not?" One of his hands ran down her arm and wound around her hand. His other cupped her cheek. "If you're planning to leave town, you're not in the market for anything serious either. We already like each other. We're already spending a lot of time together. Why not take the next step?"

She had the strong feeling that something in his logic was seriously flawed, but she couldn't figure out what it was.

She said the first thing that popped into her mind. "You just view me as a challenge because I don't want to date you."

"You know me better than that." He was right. She did. Dan had far too much integrity to chase a woman for the sole purpose of determining whether he could catch her. "Besides, you do want to date me."

"Is that right?"

His hands moved to her waist. Before she could guess his intentions, he hoisted her onto the washing machine so that their height difference was minimized.

"That's right." His eyes moved over her mouth. She felt her heartbeat speed up. He took a step forward so her legs hung on either side of him, with their upper bodies almost touching. "You want to kiss me, too."

She started to deny it, then realized here was a chance to tell the truth. "So what if I do?"

He grinned. "So let's stop denying what we both want."

"I want—" she was touching him, too, her hands running over his hard chest "—to keep things casual."

He stared into her eyes. "Then we'll keep things casual."

They moved forward at the same time, their mouths coming together hungrily. She'd kissed him only twice, but both times had been so memorable that she knew exactly how to slant her head and open her mouth to get the most out of the experience. She held his head in place, trying to get closer, wishing they were skin to skin.

She felt as though she couldn't get enough of him. Not of his scent, those hard lips that instantly softened upon contact or the passion that could flare between them so quickly.

On the heels of that thought came a crazier one—that she'd never get enough of him.

Through the haze of her senses, she heard an abrupt sound she probably should have been able to identify.

"Oh, I'm sorry!" The declaration was loud and unexpected and gave a strong clue that the sound had been a door opening. "I didn't mean to interrupt."

Jill reluctantly turned away from Dan's mouth and toward the door that now stood ajar. Sara Brenneman stood stock-still at the entrance to the laundry room, her gaze dipping to Dan's hand, which was on Jill's left breast.

"I didn't know anyone was in here." Sara was usually the epitome of cool, but she was almost stammering. "I thought this was the restroom."

Without another word, Sara closed the door.

Jill stared at Dan, then leaned her forehead weakly against his. She could hear his heart beating, or was that hers?

"We might as well give in and start dating," she said, her voice coming in fits and starts, "because our deniability is shot."

JILL STOOD OUTSIDE the discount department store an hour's drive from Indigo Springs early on Monday afternoon, her back to a brick wall on the side of the building where hardly anyone parked.

On her prepaid cell phone she punched in a telephone number she knew by heart. Her index finger flew over the keys so quickly she hit a wrong number. She tried again and made another mistake.

"Slow down, Jill," she told herself aloud. On her third try, she got the number right.

"Hello?" The greeting was tentative.

"Mama. It's Jill."

"Jill! I am so happy to hear from you." Her mother's familiar voice came over the line, sending warmth and love flowing through Jill. "But we talked only a couple weeks ago. Is something wrong?"

"Nothing's wrong." Jill never called from Indigo Springs, phoning only during her monthly trip to stock up on toiletries and paper products. This time, she'd waited only two weeks between visits to the store. "Quite the opposite, actually. I've met somebody."

Jill almost giggled at how eager she was to blurt out the news. It had been that way when she was a teenager, too. When something notable happened in her life, she couldn't wait to tell her mother.

"That's wonderful, Jill!" Her mother reacted with the wholehearted happiness that made sharing good news with her such a joy. "I want to hear all about him."

Jill leaned her back against the wall and closed her eyes, wondering how best to describe Dan Maguire.

"Let's see. He's kind and generous and so likable he even won over Chris. He's a mountain biker, although I don't think a very dedicated one. He's the vet everybody wants to treat their pets, but his dogs aren't well behaved." She laughed. "You should hear those dogs bark when someone comes to the door. It hurts your ears. But that's because Dan enjoys being around them so much he's too soft on them, which shows you what a good heart he has."

"That's all well and good—" her mother's voice held a smile "—but is this Dan hot?"

"Oh, yeah!" Jill pictured Dan the way he'd looked Sunday night when they agreed to start seeing each other. "He's Irish, with hair as black as mine, fair skin and these gorgeous blue eyes. Tall and lean but not skinny. And he has this great, deep voice."

"How long have you been going out?"

"Let's see." Jill checked her wristwatch, confirming it was nearly two in the afternoon. She'd sandwiched this trip to the store between her morning white water run and her shift at the Blue Haven. "About fifteen hours."

"You just met him?" her mother asked.

"Oh, no. We were both at a party last night, and that's when we decided to start dating." She smiled at the thought of the laundry room, a memory so vivid she could almost smell the detergent and feel Dan's lips on hers. That was as intimate as they'd gotten. After the party broke up, he'd driven her straight to Chase and Kelly's to pick up Chris. "But we've been friends for a while."

"The best relationships start as friendships," her mother said. "So I guess this means you've told him about Chris."

Jill stopped smiling. "I haven't told anyone about Chris. I can't."

"You just said you and Dan were friends."

"That has nothing to do with it," Jill said. "You know what happened with Ray. It never occurred to me he'd tell Daddy what I was planning. I learned the best way to keep Chris safe is to say nothing."

"So what do you say when Dan asks about your past?"

"I tell him as much of the truth as I can." Jill swallowed, thinking about the lie she'd relayed about her father being dead. "At the same time, I say as little as possible."

"Oh, honey." Her mother's words held a wealth of feeling. "I'm so sorry."

"It can't be helped," Jill said. "I can't afford to make even one more mistake."

She heard what sounded like her mother blowing out a breath. "Unfortunately, you could be right. There's something I have to tell you, too. Your father called me again a few days ago."

"Is he still with Arianne?" Jill asked the question every time she and her mother talked, although she was always fairly sure of the answer.

"He's still sticking by her," her mother said. "I swear, that woman has your father completely fooled. I only met her the one time and it seems pretty clear to me she's a phony who married him for his money."

"Why did Daddy call you?" Jill's hand clenched into a fist at her side. Although her parents managed to be civil, they generally avoided each other. The only thing they had in common, her mother often said, was Jill.

"He wanted me to tell you your time is running out," her mother said. "He feels like you've backed him into a corner, so he's giving you an ultimatum. If you don't bring Chris back before two weeks is up, he's going to the police."

Jill felt the thump-thump-thump of her heart speeding up. "I'll come back tomorrow if he kicks Arianne out of the house."

"We both know that's not going to happen. The woman can do no wrong in his eyes."

"Then the answer's no," Jill said. "I'm not putting Chris at risk. No matter what."

"Your father says the police have access to more re-sources than a private eye," her mother said. "He says it would only be a matter of time before they found you."

Jill's stomach knotted and her chest tightened, but she raised her chin. "We'll see about that."

Her mother was silent for a few beats. "This Dan you were telling me about—you're not in love with him, are you?"

It was too early for Jill to put a label on her feelings. Or maybe she hadn't put a name on them because cau-tion had become the watchword in her life.

She didn't need her mother to tell her the inevitable. That the only outcome to the situation her father had thrust her into spelled the end of her relationship.

Either she and Chris left Indigo Springs before the cops got close. Or she stayed too long, dooming Chris to life with a cruel witch in designer clothing and herself to a possible jail sentence.

"No. I can't afford to fall in love," Jill said.

CHAPTER TEN

"YOU POUR ME A DRINK or I'll come back there and make you pour!"

The drunk's threat cut through all the other noise in the Blue Haven on Tuesday evening as Dan entered the bar.

The man was a behemoth, weighing more than three hundred pounds and topping six feet by a good four or five inches. He was looming over the bar, and one of his hands was balled into a fist, his anger a dark palpable force directed behind the bar.

At Jill.

Adrenaline coursed through Dan. He rushed forward, almost careening into a man rising from his chair.

"Sorry," he mumbled, but kept going, his eyes on the scene unfolding at the bar.

"You don't mean that, darlin'." Jill's expression was pleasant, her posture fully relaxed, her voice soft. "You know the reason I won't pour you another beer is because I'm looking out for you."

"Yesh, I do mean it!" the drunk yelled, slurring his words. "You do what I shay! Or...or..."

"Or nothing." Jill actually took a step closer to him and leaned over the bar. "We both know you're too good of a guy to ever hurt your favorite bartender."

All the anger seeped out of the man, as though

someone had deflated a balloon. Dan stopped in his tracks, hardly believing what he was seeing.

"Shorry." The man bowed his head, sounding ashamed. "But I shtill want a beer."

"And I'm still not giving you one," Jill said. "I'll tell you what I can do, though. I can give your brother a call and get you a ride home. You're still living with Pete, right?"

"No need to bother Pete." Another man rose from his stool, his movements and speech marking him as sober. "I was just leaving. I can give him a ride. C'mon, Big Ron."

The drunk man shuffled obediently behind him, all the fight gone from him.

Jill looked up and spotted Dan. Surprise registered on her face, which was more emotion than she'd shown when dealing with Big Ron. "Hey, Dan. What are you doing here?"

"I dropped by to say hello."

"At eleven-thirty?" Her eyebrows rose and disappeared under her curly hair. Her clothes were subdued by Jill standards, a T-shirt with a starburst design paired with faded blue jeans. Her only jewelry consisted of a watch and huge blue hoop earrings. She looked delectable. "Don't you have to get up early tomorrow for work?"

Since the party on Sunday night, he hadn't seen her at all. Either she'd been working or he had. She normally had Tuesday nights off, but had traded shifts with another bartender in order to attend the party.

"It's worth losing sleep to see you," he said, a line that didn't get him the smile he was shooting for. He winked at her. "I said that just in case you liked a smooth-talking man."

Her lips curved.

Only a few of the stools around the bar were taken. He settled onto an empty one and nodded in the direction the departing men had taken. "What was that all about?"

She looked at him blankly.

"The big guy yelling threats at you," he clarified. "I was headed over here to defend you." Recalling the guy's size, he quirked one side of his mouth. "Or, at least, to try to defend you."

"From Big Ron?" Jill shook her head. "Big Ron is harmless."

"He didn't sound harmless when he was trying to bully you into pouring him a beer."

"He gets like that about once a month when we cut him off," Jill said. "I don't take it personally. He'll be in here tomorrow apologizing all over himself."

"Sounds like a bar isn't the best place for him to hang out," Dan said.

"Maybe, except that's never gonna change," Jill said. "Big Ron thinks of the other regulars as family. He can hold his booze most of the time. He's just upset today because he got word his son has bronchitis and isn't coming to visit. His son's thirteen. He lives in California with Big Ron's ex."

"How do you know all that?" he asked.

"Are you kidding me? A good bartender specializes in listening. The job's only ten percent about making drinks." She slapped her palms on the bar. "So what can I get you?"

"Whatever ale you have on tap," he said. "High-test, not unloaded."

"Just to be clear, that means no light beer, right?"

So much for trying to be a smooth talker. "Right," he said.

Although there was a smattering of people at the tables, the crowd was light, with nobody clamoring for her attention.

"Where is everybody tonight?" he asked.

"Tuesdays have been slow since Chuck started staying open on Mondays." She took a tall glass from a shelf behind her. "He switched out Two for Tuesdays for Maniac Mondays. It thinned out the crowd so much that now he's thinking of closing on Tuesdays."

"I'm in favor of anything that'll give you more free time."

"Free time? What's that?" She tilted the glass under the tap and filled it with pale ale, leaving a thin layer of foam at the top. "Here you go."

She set the glass down before he could take it from her. He got the impression she didn't want to risk physical contact, even if it was the merest brushing of fingers. But that was crazy. Two nights ago they'd decided to see where their attraction would lead.

"Where'd you learn how to bartend anyway?" he asked.

"On-the-job training," she said. "School wasn't for me, not even bartending school."

"And?" he asked when she didn't elaborate.

"And by the time I graduated high school, I was sick of waitressing. So I nagged my boss until he let me learn the ropes behind the bar."

"Was this in South Carolina?" he asked.

"That's right."

He couldn't remember her ever naming a specific town where she'd lived. "Whereabouts in South Carolina?"

"Oh, here and there," she said airily. "I told you I lived with my mama, right? We moved around."

"Even after high school?"

"By then it was a habit. Be right back." She moved away before he could ask more questions, adding to his feeling that she wasn't particularly glad to see him. Or perhaps she didn't realize that no detail about her past was too small, even a listing of all the places she'd lived.

He watched her check to see if the two other people sitting at the bar wanted a refill. They were a young couple not much older than the legal drinking age. They shook their heads, barely taking their eyes off each other.

She headed back his way, her hoop earrings swinging.

"I don't have any bartending experience," Dan said, "but I'd say that couple wants to be left alone."

"You got that right," she said, then…silence.

"I saw Chris today," Dan said. "He came by to visit the goats, the same as always. After a while he pulled this crumpled piece of paper out of his pocket and handed it to me. It was an invitation to a birthday party."

Her expression brightened. Finally he'd sparked her interest. "Did you get the impression he wanted to go?"

"Yeah, I did. Why?"

"Chris didn't even know who Timmy Waverly was until I told him he was Brittany's brother," Jill said. "Apparently Timmy didn't say a word to Chris while we were at Hershey."

"They why did Timmy invite Chris to his birthday party?"

"My guess is his mother did the guest list," Jill said. "Chris and Brittany hit it off so well, she might have invited Chris so Brittany has someone to hang out with."

"That could be true," Dan said, "but this is a chance for Chris to get to know some of the boys better."

"Exactly what I told him," Jill said. "Thank God the party's at the miniature golf course."

"Yeah, Chris told me he's pretty good at mini golf."

"He's darn near a ringer," she said. "I've taken him a few times, and he always beats me."

"You and I should go this weekend. I'm not bad." Dan smiled at her. "Maybe I could coach you up."

"You can coach me up some other time," she said, repeating the phrase with the same Southern flair he'd given it. "I'm busy this weekend."

"Don't you have Friday night off?"

"Not this week," she said. "I'm working Friday so I can get Saturday night off. You know that bike race proposal? I'm going to Lake Wallenpaupack on Saturday to present it."

"Then maybe we can go out Saturday night when you get back."

"My appointment isn't until the late afternoon," she said, "so I'm not sure when I'll be back."

"Why don't I come to Lake Wallenpaupack with you?" As soon as he came up with the notion, he knew it was the right one. "We can even make a weekend of it. What do you say? Can Indigo River Rafters do without you on Sunday morning?"

"That's not such a good idea. It's just that…" She didn't seem to know how to proceed, which was unlike her. "When you think about it, it would be our first official date. It just seems a bit, well, *intense* for a first date."

He looked around, then lowered his voice. "We can get separate rooms. I should have made that clear."

"We'd still be staying overnight," she said. "I'm just not comfortable with that."

"Then let's make it a day trip."

She winced. "I think I'm just gonna go on up there alone. I'll be so nervous about the presentation, I'd probably be lousy company anyway."

He refrained from pointing out that he could help calm her nerves, that she could even practice her pitch on him during the drive up.

"Jill," Chuck Dudza, the bar owner, called. "Can you come over here a minute?"

"Sure, boss," she said with alacrity. To Dan, she added, "Be right back."

He rewound the conversation, trying to figure out where he'd taken a wrong turn. He'd had the vague impression Jill wasn't particularly glad to see him, but it had gotten worse when he'd mentioned an overnight trip.

"It's slow tonight," Chuck remarked to Jill. He wasn't

talking loudly, but his voice carried to Dan. "You want to take off early?"

"Oh, no," Jill answered quickly. "You go ahead. I'll close up."

In his peripheral vision, Dan saw Chuck shoot him a pointed glance that Jill couldn't have missed. "You sure?"

"Absolutely." Jill's head bobbed. "You closed for me last week. It's my turn."

Dan got the hint. He finished the last of his beer and stood up. "I'm taking off," he called to Jill.

She walked over to him, her face a polite mask. "Probably a smart idea. I'll be here a while."

"Walk me out?" he asked.

"Go ahead, Jill," Chuck interjected before she could answer. Her boss was at the sink, rinsing dishes, watching their interaction. "I'm not leaving for at least ten more minutes."

Long moments passed before Jill nodded. When they were outside the bar, she kept a few feet between them. He motioned her away from the well-lit bar to the front of a darkened store, feeling the need to set things right.

"I'm sorry about what just happened in there." He put his hands on either side of her shoulders. "I swear to you, I didn't suggest I come with you on Saturday so I could get you in bed."

"I—"

He covered her lips with three fingers. "Let me finish. It's not that I don't want to sleep with you. Nothing could be further from the truth. But I won't rush you. I promise. We can go entirely at your pace."

She gazed up at him. The spot where he'd led her was so dark that all he could make out of her eyes were the whites. He couldn't see any nuances of her expression.

She said nothing for so long he thought she was devising a way to tell him she'd changed her mind about dating him. Just when he was about to make another plea for understanding, she grabbed the front of his shirt, stood on tiptoe and kissed him.

The heat of the kiss enveloped him, the passion accelerating like a sports car going from cruising speed to eighty miles per hour. She kissed him as she had in the laundry room but with more desperation, as though she'd been waiting to get him alone again.

He knew the feeling. He accommodated her, slanting his mouth over hers, meeting the thrusts of her tongue with his own. Never in his thirty years had he ever wanted a woman this badly. Not even Maggie.

And then the kiss was over. She stepped back, out of his arms, her face and body in shadows. There was enough ambient light, however, that he could see her chest heaving.

"Good night, Dan." Her words were breathy.

"Good night."

She whirled and headed quickly toward the bar, disappearing inside and leaving him to wonder what that had been all about. One moment, she'd seemed to be distancing herself from him. The next, she hadn't been able to get close enough.

He was certain of one thing, however. If kisses like that were his reward, he was prepared to be patient for a very, very long time.

JILL PEEKED THROUGH the branches of a low-hanging tree late on Saturday morning, repositioning herself until the foursome of young boys was in her sight line.

She'd been wrong about Chris being invited to the birthday party to keep Brittany company. The delightful little blonde was playing the hole with the leaping dolphins, joined by three other equally cute girls.

Chris's golf partners were all boys she recognized from the trip to Hershey. They were talking and laughing among themselves while Chris silently went about the business of miniature golf, lining up his putts, slowing bringing back the club, stroking through the ball.

"What are you doing behind this tree?" a low voice asked.

Jill gasped. Her heartbeat sped up, her body jerked, her hand flying to her throat as she turned.

It was Dan.

"Sorry if I scared you," he said.

She was over the shock. Her heartbeat, though, hadn't slowed a tick. If anything, it had sped up.

She'd never seen him in so little clothing. He was dressed in a loose-fitting sleeveless T-shirt, running shorts and athletic shoes. Her eyes headed south to his legs before jerking upward.

"Shouldn't you be at work?" she asked, although she knew the answer. The veterinarian's office was open until noon every Saturday.

"We had some cancellations, so Stanley chased me out the door." He wasn't breathing hard, although he was obviously out for a run. "I'm glad he did. Otherwise I'd never have spotted you hiding in the bushes."

"It's not a bush," she denied strongly before the

ridiculousness of the situation struck her. She giggled. "It's a tree, and I'm hiding so Chris doesn't know I'm spying on him."

"Makes perfect sense." His eyes crinkled so they were smiling. "Why exactly are you spying on him?"

"I thought about standing at the fence and waving at him," she said. "Except he's probably at the age where he'd be mortified to have his big sister hovering over him."

"That sounds right," Dan said. "Except you still haven't told me why his big sister is hovering over him."

She winced. "To see how the party's going. I could tell he was nervous about it this morning, so I got nervous, too."

"How is it going?" Dan came forward so they were side by side. He was perspiring lightly, but smelled clean, like the outdoors.

"He's in a group with three other boys. I haven't been here long, but so far he hasn't said a word to any of them." Jill moved the branch aside once more to get a better view.

"Allow me," Dan said, holding it in place for her.

Chris and the other members of his foursome had moved to the next hole, which involved directing the ball through a revolving windmill. Chris was up first, which meant he must have had the low score on the previous hole.

The other boys hung back talking and laughing while Chris set his bright yellow ball down on the rubber square. After careful consideration, which was how her brother did everything, he stroked through the ball.

The yellow sphere traveled over the green carpet, shot through an opening in the windmill and kept going in a straight line to the hole. It disappeared into the cup.

"Hole in one!" one of the boys in Chris's foursome yelled, his voice carrying to their hiding place.

"Way to go, man!" yelled another.

The boys surrounded Chris, slapping him on the back and awarding him high fives. Jill and Dan were perhaps forty feet away, but Jill still saw her brother's white teeth flash.

"I'd say he's doing just fine," Dan said, letting the branch fall back into place.

"He is, isn't he?" Jill smiled. Finally, after more than a year on the run, her brother seemed to be on the verge of making friends his own age. He'd even stopped offering profuse apologies for every minor mistake. "I guess this means I can go."

"I'm sort of surprised you're still here in Indigo Springs," Dan said. "Aren't you submitting that proposal today?"

"I sure am," Jill said. "It's not a long drive—ninety minutes at most. I don't have to leave until after lunch."

She waited for him to repeat his offer to accompany her.

"Are you prepared?" he asked instead.

"No," she said, "but I'll muddle through it."

He merely nodded in acknowledgment.

"Felicia let me practice on her this morning and she said I did fine," Jill said.

He cocked his head. "Just *fine?*"

"She actually said I did terrific, except she's biased,"

Jill said. "Felicia's teaching me how to cook some of her specialties. No matter how much I mess up, she always says the food tastes delicious."

"We all need someone like that in our lives," he said.

She could be that person in Dan's life. The thought struck her like a bolt of lightning. She'd gushed about him to her mother, yet had guarded against letting him know how great a guy she thought he was.

She'd gone out of her way, in fact, to distance herself from him. Tuesday night was the latest example. Discounting the impulsive kiss she'd given him outside the bar, she'd been deliberately standoffish. All because of the revelation that her father was getting ready to call in the cops.

"I should be getting back to my run." His eyes lingered on her the same way they always did, but his smile was almost impersonal. "Good luck with the presentation."

He turned and left her, starting a slow jog that would take him farther and farther away.

"Wait!" she called, breaking into her own run, desperate to close the distance she'd created between them.

He stopped and turned, a puzzled look on his face. "Did you want something?"

She wanted *him*, which must have been evident outside the bar Tuesday night. Yet he'd made no move to follow up on that implicit invitation.

Wednesday had rolled around, turning into Thursday and then Friday with no word from him. Her days and nights had been filled with work, yes, but she could have at least fit in a lunch with him.

"Why haven't you called?" she asked.

He shielded his eyes from the sun. "I thought it was obvious."

She shook her head.

"This is me not pressuring you," he said. "If it were up to me, we'd be moving at warp speed. But I meant what I said. I'm willing to go at your pace."

She couldn't imagine another man who'd been kissed the way she'd kissed Dan on Tuesday night being as understanding.

Then again, it became clearer to her by the day that in Dan she'd found someone special.

She'd told her mother she couldn't afford to fall in love with him. The real question was whether she could pass up the chance to see where things between them might lead.

It didn't have to end with her leaving town. Even if her father did go to the police, that didn't mean the law would find them. She and Chris had been in Indigo Springs for almost a year. The town might be the best place to hide.

"What are you doing for the rest of the weekend?" she asked abruptly.

"Let's see. After I finish my run, I was thinking about a shower." He shrugged. "And that's about the extent of my plans. Why?"

"If I can find someone to fill in for me tomorrow morning at Indigo River Rafters, what do you say to taking that weekend trip after all?"

"How soon would I need to be ready to go?" he asked.

"An hour," she said. "Can you do that?"

"Just watch me." He took off at a dead run, calling over his shoulder as he went, "Not that I'm too eager."

She laughed, something breaking free inside her.

She realized it was hope.

CHAPTER ELEVEN

THE RACE DIRECTOR of the Poconos Challenge was a small, wiry man with a mustache, barely contained enthusiasm and a face Jill had never seen before in her life.

Equally unfamiliar were the two assistants who sat on either side of Wayne Harrison, smiling and nodding along with the race director as Jill finished her presentation.

Wayne grinned hugely. The sight was even more welcome than the view of Lake Wallenpaupack visible through the window of the meeting room. The Eagle Eye resort had lived up to its "luxury on the lake" billing, in no small part because a savvy architect had designed the building to showcase views of the lake. It was easy to see why the Poconos Challenge organizers had chosen the site to begin and end their event.

"Well done!" Wayne said. "That was our most entertaining proposal of the day."

Jill had had a feeling things would go well when she'd arrived and verified that all three of the organizers were strangers. She'd known it was unlikely the tendrils of the racing community would extend from Georgia to a resort in the Poconos. Her anxiety hadn't disappeared, however, until she'd confirmed that.

"Which part?" Jill asked. "When I couldn't do the PowerPoint without help or the slide I snuck in of the pygmy goats?"

"All of it," said the older of the two assistant directors, a balding man wearing a yellow racing jersey. "You made Indigo Springs sound like a fun destination."

"Makes me wonder why I've never paid the town a visit," added the only female member of the committee. She was small, soft-spoken and probably the woman who'd gone to pharmacy school with Chad Armstrong.

"If you choose our beautiful town as one of your lucky finalists, you can change that." Jill sounded like a walking advertisement, which wasn't her style. She consoled herself that she might be helping Chad further a romance. "Tell you what. Bring your bikes along, and I'll lead a ride."

"We'd love that," Wayne said, lending credence to Charlie Bradford's theory that cyclists related best to their own kind. Wayne stood up, and the other two did the same. "You can bet you'll be hearing from us."

"Great!" Jill went forward to shake their hands in turn. She took her time, although she really wanted to rush out of the room to share the news with Dan.

He'd suggested she run through the presentation during the drive from Indigo Springs, listening with a critical ear and giving her a major suggestion on how to improve it: get rid of the note cards and just talk.

She could hardly wait to tell him the casual approach had worked. To be truthful, she'd have been eager to join him even if it hadn't.

He'd offered to check them in to the resort while she presented the case for Indigo Springs. Once she left this meeting room, the truly adventurous part of her weekend would start.

Someone rapped on the door, then flung it open. A woman about her age with a beautiful shade of red hair stuck her head into the room.

"Sorry." The woman grimaced. "I was just checking to see if you were done with the room."

"Don't go, Sally," Wayne called. "We're just finishing up now. Come in and meet Jill Jacobi. She just submitted a proposal."

The woman, beautifully dressed in a baby-blue linen business suit, stepped into the room. She was tall, thin—and shockingly familiar.

Jill's heart came to a crashing stop. Or at least it felt as though it did. She wasn't sure where she'd seen the woman before, but something about her long, thin nose and severely arched brows struck a chord.

"Sally Tomlin, this is Jill Jacobi." Wayne made the introductions while Jill tried to remember if she'd heard the name before. "Jill, Sally works in the resort's marketing department. She's a mountain biker, too, so she's acting as liaison between her people and our people."

Jill's fears had come true. The woman was part of the cycling community. Yet Jill could be mistaken about recognizing her. She certainly would have remembered had she seen that particular shade of red before.

"Nice to meet you, Jill." Sally stuck out a hand, her manner professional. Before Jill could take it, she cocked her head and narrowed her eyes. "Have we met before?"

Jill took the other woman's hand, racking her brain, trying to figure out why the other woman seemed familiar. "Not that I can recall."

"I know I've seen you before," Sally said as they shook hands.

Jill swallowed. Was Sally from Atlanta? Jill thought she detected a slight rounding of the vowels that hinted she might be a native Southerner.

"Have you ever been to Indigo Springs?" Wayne asked. "Jill's a bartender there."

Sally snapped her slender fingers. "That must be it. I love that little town. My husband and I have been there a couple of times."

Relief poured through Jill, and she felt as though her blood was circulating again. "There you go."

Although she didn't specifically remember Sally from the Blue Haven, that must be why she seemed familiar. Tourists came and tourists went, rotating through the bar as though it had a revolving door.

"I don't mean to rush you," Sally said, addressing the three men, "but I'm headed home. If you're not through, you can ask someone at the front desk to lock up the meeting room."

"Oh, no, no," Wayne said. "We're all finished here. I'm sure Jill is eager to get on with her day."

Wayne had that right, Jill thought after she left the meeting, switched on her cell phone and saw a text from Dan that read Meet me in room 402.

She hurried through the plush resort, passing an indoor pool, sauna and fitness facility before she reached the lobby. A couple and their three children were waiting for the elevator. Jill bypassed them and took the steps, rushing up them so fast she nearly stumbled.

"Slow down," she told herself between the third and fourth floors. She couldn't seem to take her own advice, finding herself in front of room 402 in practically no time at all.

She didn't hesitate, rapping lightly on the door. It swung open almost immediately. The elegant room didn't take her breath away. Dan did. She'd already seen him that afternoon, of course, but was struck again by how good he looked. Unlike her, he was dressed in casual clothes—khaki shorts, sandals and a white shirt that made his black hair seem even darker.

"Well?" he asked, an expectant gleam in his eyes. "How did it go?"

"It went great," she said. "They all but told me Indigo Springs would be one of the finalists."

"See. All that worrying for nothing."

She had a fleeting thought of the panic she'd felt upon meeting Sally Tomlin, then banished the woman from her mind. The mystery of why Sally seemed familiar had been solved.

"For nothing," she repeated. She walked deeper into the beautifully appointed guest room, decorated in warm shades of peach coupled with mahogany furniture. A window seat overlooked the lake, its water still glistening even though there were only a few hours of daylight remaining. "This is gorgeous."

She finally let her eyes rest on the focal point of the room, a king-size canopy bed with a lacy white bedspread.

Her heartbeat sped up.

She should be annoyed that he'd asked for a room with a king-size bed after he'd made a point of saying they'd move at her pace. Yet she was oddly excited.

"I have a surprise for you," he said, "but first you have to change out of those clothes."

She thought of the little black dress she'd packed, then the skimpy nightgown. Which one was he suggesting?

"You brought sneakers, right?" He didn't wait for her acknowledgment. "Make sure you wear those. We don't have much daylight left. Can you meet me in ten minutes?"

She wouldn't feel comfortable getting undressed in front of him before they shared a bed, but she could change her clothes in the spacious bathroom.

"Meet you where?" she asked.

"Outside in the hall," he said. "I'm next door in room 404. You can knock when you're ready."

"Seriously?" She felt her mouth drop open. "You got two rooms?"

He smiled, bent down, then kissed her open mouth, softly and sweetly. The kiss was over far too soon. He stroked her cheek.

"I told you I wouldn't rush you." He stepped away, and it took all her restraint not to grab for him and yank him back. "Ten minutes. Be ready."

She was already ready, she realized after he left the room. When they'd left Indigo Springs she hadn't been sure how far she'd let their relationship progress.

Now she was sure.

She was going to make love to him.

Tonight.

SLOW AND STEADY, Dan told himself as he navigated his pickup truck through the narrow, twisting paved road just north of Lake Wallenpaupack, keeping an eye out for the iron bridge.

It came into view beyond a steep curve. He tapped on the brakes and made a hard left onto a gravel road. Almost immediately the road ascended steeply.

Slow and steady, he repeated silently.

The phrase applied to more than just his driving. Taking things slowly with Jill was a good idea, and not only because she was skittish. Given his own romantic history, proceeding with caution was the right course of action.

"Why haven't you asked where we're going?" he asked. Since they'd set out on the ten-mile trip, she'd been content to talk of inconsequential things.

"And ruin the surprise?" she asked. "No way!"

He risked a glance at Jill even though the pickup was climbing the road at a steep angle, tires crunching as it labored uphill. She was sitting slightly forward in her seat, and the corners of her mouth were turned up. She wore shorts and a red sleeveless top that showed off her toned arms. Her hair was soft and loose, the way he liked it.

After about a half mile, the road flattened out and ended in a small empty parking lot.

She hopped out of the truck almost the instant it stopped. He was slower to join her, first snatching his backpack from the rear seat. By the time he slung it over his shoulder, she was having a hard time standing still.

"You must really like surprises," he said, amused.

"Like them?" she repeated. "I love them! So lead the way."

He surveyed the area, almost immediately locating the trampled grass that signaled a path. "I think it's that way."

"You don't know for sure?"

"I've never been here before." He walked ahead of her down a path that didn't seem as though it had seen much use in recent days.

A telltale gurgling sound that grew louder with each passing step, however, told him they were heading in the right direction. She must have figured it out, too. When the path widened, she drew even with him and grinned.

"C'mon, slowpoke." She took his hand, increasing their traveling speed twofold although he'd been going at a decent clip.

The brush thinned out and the sky brightened, affording a clear view of a waterfall. The rocks were positioned in tiers, like the wedding cake at the party for Kelly and Chase Bradford. The water cascaded over the stones, dropping into a clear stream perhaps twenty feet below.

"I love it!" Jill threw her arms open, as though trying to embrace the scene. "How did you know this waterfall was here?"

"A guy I rode the elevator with at the resort told me about it," Dan said. "He called it a hidden gem."

"Let's get a closer look." She scampered a few feet downhill to a large flat rock and got close to the edge. "The view's prettier from here. I can even feel some spray."

When her back was turned, he set down his backpack,

removed a red-and-white-checkered tablecloth and spread it with a flourish.

She pivoted. "What's this?" she asked, her eyes smiling.

"This is a picnic." He sat down on the tablecloth, rummaged through his backpack and produced a bottle of cabernet sauvignon, two plastic glasses, a box of crackers and spreadable cheese. "A wine-and-cheese picnic, to be specific. I thought about take-out food, but if you'd smelled it the surprise would have been ruined."

"It's perfect!" She sat down beside him and tucked her legs under her. They both had a view of the waterfall, but he thought his vantage point was better because it included her. "Did you bring all this with you from home?"

"Only the corkscrew." He pulled the item from his backpack. "The resort has a well-stocked gift shop."

"Easy access to your own personal corkscrew is a very good idea," she said as he opened the bottle.

"I have my big sister to thank for that. She says it's hard to resist a man wielding a bottle of wine on a picnic." Dan made googly eyes at her, and she laughed.

He poured wine into the two glasses, then handed one to her. "What should we drink to?"

"I know," she said, lifting her glass. "To happiness."

"To happiness," he repeated, lightly clinking his glass to hers. He took a sip, then opened the cheese and crackers, arranging them on a paper plate the gift-shop clerk had also suggested he buy.

She bit into a cracker, followed it with wine, then asked, "Does your sister often give you advice?"

"*Often?* Try *always*." He stretched his legs out in front of him and crossed them at the ankles. "And it's not only one sister telling me what to do—it's three. My youngest sister is seven years older than me."

"I'm sure they mean well."

"Oh, they do. Sometimes they're even right. Karen—that's my oldest sister—figured out I should become a veterinarian before I did. It's when they start giving out romantic advice that they go too far."

"What kind of romantic advice?"

"Let's see." He thought of the last conversation he'd had with Karen. "No. I can't tell you that."

"Sure, you can," she said. "How else am I going to get to know you better?"

He shrugged. "Okay. Karen thinks I should invite you to come with me to my cousin Nancy's wedding in Ohio."

She gasped softly. "You told your sister about me?"

"Not you, specifically," he said. "I told my sister I met somebody I liked. She took it from there, disregarding that I'm not even going to the wedding."

"Why not?" she asked.

He'd already said too much, but there was no going back now that he'd brought up the subject.

"Nancy is marrying my ex's brother," he said. "Maggie, that's my ex, is bringing her new husband to the wedding."

"You're not going because you don't want to run into her," Jill finished. It was a statement, not a question.

Dan let the words sink in. They sounded wrong even though they'd been true a few weeks ago. He realized a lot had changed since then.

"I don't care if I run into her," he said.

"You don't?" Jill tilted her head. "Then you are going to the wedding?"

"I think I am." He wasn't a man who often changed his mind once he made a decision. But then, he realized, he was no longer a man with a broken heart. "I might even take Karen's advice and ask you to come with me."

"Oh, really?" She didn't say no, which he took as a good sign. "What will determine whether you ask me or not?"

"I'm waiting to see how this weekend goes," he said.

They'd both finished the wine in their glasses. She set hers down and took his empty glass from him. Without breaking eye contact, she inched closer to him.

"I predict," she said softly, her gaze dropping to his mouth, "that your weekend's about to get a whole lot better."

Then she kissed him, her lips moving eagerly over his. She tasted of the wine she'd drunk and the cheese and crackers she'd eaten. He didn't intend to have more than one glass of wine because he had to navigate the twisting road back to the resort, but he could get drunk on her.

They kissed hungrily, their hands sliding over each other, their bodies shifting in an effort to get closer. He pulled her into his lap, where she couldn't mistake his arousal.

He kissed the side of her lips, her cheek, her neck. "Maybe we should stop," he murmured.

"Why?" Her voice was breathy. "Nobody's here but us."

"The light," he said. "It's fading."

She drew back from him. Her eyes were glazed but they also contained a healthy dose of mischievousness.

"Less chance of anyone seeing us if they do come along," she said.

He felt his eyebrows rise and his heart lift. "Really?"

"Did you bring protection?" she asked, erasing any doubt of her meaning.

"In my wallet," he said.

"Then really." She pulled her shirt over her head, her dark hair tumbling to her bare shoulders. Her breasts were small and perfectly shaped, her nipples already taut. A siren's smile played about her lips.

With the water tumbling over the rocks behind her and the setting sun above casting her in a soft light, he thought he'd never seen a lovelier sight.

He took a mental snapshot, already aware he'd remember this moment forever. Slow and steady was overrated, he thought as he reached for happiness.

JILL COULD IMAGINE few things more pleasurable than waking up in a luxury hotel room with a stunning view of a Poconos lake and Dan Maguire naked in bed next to her.

She was snuggled against him, his body warming her. He looked sexy in sleep, the dark sweep of his lashes matching his morning stubble. The white sheet had slipped to his waist, and his bare, hair-sprinkled chest expanded and contracted as he drew in deep, regular breaths.

Those dark lashes lifted, revealing the clear blue of

his irises. His eyes softened and he smiled lazily. "Good morning."

She smiled back. "You betcha."

They both moved forward, their mouths meeting in a soft, slow kiss without a trace of awkwardness. They'd discovered the previous day and night that their bodies fit together, their rhythms matched and the passion between them was effortless.

So was the companionship. After the trip to the waterfall, they'd dined by candlelight in the resort's five-star restaurant and enjoyed a comedy show in the lounge before returning to the room.

"Mmmm," she said when they both broke for air, "I sure am glad you didn't insist on going back to your own room last night."

Tendrils of hair had fallen into her face. He smoothed them back with gentle fingers. "Didn't you beg me not to?"

"I probably would have gotten around to that," she said, "if you hadn't been doing so much begging yourself."

He laughed, then rolled over so his weight was on his knees, his body hovering above hers with his hands lightly clamping both of her wrists.

"Now that I've got you at my mercy," he said, lowering his already deep voice, "you're the one who needs to do my bidding."

She smiled invitingly up at him. "I like the sound of that. What would you like me to do?"

He didn't hesitate. "Tell me your favorite color."

She frowned. "My favorite color? I thought I was going to do your bidding."

"Then answer my question."

He stared down at her, the expression in his eyes oddly serious. They were such a pretty shade, somewhere between the color of the sky and the water of the Caribbean.

"Blue," she said.

"Favorite food?"

"Shrimp." She'd eaten it last night in scampi, a dish that was almost but not quite as good as the company. "Always has been. When I was a little girl, I'd even try to order it at McDonald's."

He grinned. "Favorite book?"

"The Princess Bride." She sighed, remembering the tale of high adventure and true love. "It's my favorite movie, too."

"Favorite song?"

She wrinkled her nose. "Why are you asking all these questions?"

"Because somehow we got off the subject last night every time the subject was you," he said.

She'd deliberately steered the conversation away from herself, but obviously not expertly.

"So I figured my best chance of getting you to talk about yourself was if I threatened to withhold sex," he continued.

She slowly traced the outline of her lips with her tongue and injected a throaty quality into her voice. "Do you really think you're that strong?"

He closed his eyes and groaned before saying, "I'm trying to be. Favorite song?"

She sighed as frustration clawed at her, privately conceding his tactic was working. The sooner she answered his questions, the sooner they could graduate to more agreeable pursuits. "It changes. Right now it's the one Kenny Grieb sang the other night. 'Forever and for Always.'"

"Town where you were born?"

She started to say Atlanta, then caught herself in time. "Savannah."

"I thought you were from South Carolina."

Lying naked underneath him, she'd forgotten her cover story. She composed as truthful an answer as she could. "I wasn't born in South Carolina. I just lived there."

"Where in South Carolina?"

"Columbia." She and Chris had briefly stayed in the capital city. He waited, obviously expecting her to continue. She remembered stating she and her mother hadn't stayed in one place for long. She would have crossed her fingers at the lie she was about to tell if he hadn't been still holding her wrists. "Sumter and Florence. Anderson, too."

"Is this so hard?" he asked.

It was. Excruciatingly so, even if her growing sexual frustration hadn't been added to the mix. Without Chris's welfare to consider, she'd tell him the truth immediately and damn the consequences to herself.

"Hard?" She wriggled beneath him, her eyes skimming down his body to the proof of his arousal. "Does that mean you're through withholding sex?"

He managed a low-throated laugh even though his

skin was rosy and his eyes slightly unfocused. "Yes." He dipped his head until his mouth was just inches from hers and whispered, "The rest of my questions can wait."

His mouth came down on hers, reigniting the passion that easily flared between them. Sensation swamped her, and she lost herself in him, forgetting all about those questions he still had.

Until later that afternoon.

Once they were out of bed, she peppered him with her own questions, even talking during their mountain bike ride. Not only was the cliché true about the best defense being a good offense, she really wanted to know the answers.

She discovered, among other things, why the dogs he'd kept as pets in the past all had such odd names. Like his current canine duo of Starsky and Hutch, Matlock, Columbo, Crockett, Tubs and Ironside had been named for TV cops.

"I feel worst for Ironside." She and Dan had returned the bikes to the resort's rental shop and walked hand in hand toward the main building. The sun shone overhead, and the lake gently lapped at the shore. "What was wrong with him?"

"Nothing," he said. "Why?"

"Wasn't he handicapped? That TV Ironside was paralyzed from the waist down, wasn't he?"

Dan chuckled. "My Ironside had a silverish marking over his nose and eyes. He could run all day. Didn't need a wheelchair at all."

He held open the door to the side entrance of the

hotel, a gentlemanly gesture that made him even more attractive. He was thoughtful, too. He'd requested a late checkout so they could shower and change clothes before returning to Indigo Springs.

They headed down a wide hallway, off which a ball-room and assorted meeting rooms were located, toward the lobby and the elevator that would take them to their rooms. This time she grabbed his hand.

"By the way, you did fine on the ride." She'd set a moderate pace that he'd had no trouble matching. "Makes me think you weren't blowing smoke about being a mountain biker after all."

"I wouldn't do that." He wouldn't, either. She had no doubt everything he'd told her about himself was the absolute truth. "My sister Erin—she's the youngest of my sisters, but no less bossy—got me involved. She's a real jock. You'll like her."

He spoke as if it were inevitable she and his sister would meet. She dared to hope it was.

"How about you?" he asked. "How did you get into mountain biking?"

"My father." She answered the question without fore-thought, personally raising the subject she was desperate not to discuss. Now that she'd brought up her father, however, she had no choice but to elaborate. "He got me into mountain biking so we'd have something in common. Every weekend he had custody, we'd go for a ride."

"Did you love it right away?" he asked.

"Right away," she confirmed. "Daddy went out of

his way to make things fun for me. He even organized a few father-daughter rides."

"Sounds like a great thing to do with your little girl," Dan remarked.

"I was a big girl by then," she said. "The last ride was only about three or four years ago."

They'd drawn even with the meeting room where Jill had presented the proposal the day before. She got a mental flash of Sally Tomlin, the resort's marketing representative, sticking her head around the frame of the door.

Recognition jolted her, harder this time. Because she remembered where she knew Sally Tomlin from, and it wasn't the Blue Haven.

"Oh, no!" she exclaimed.

Dan stopped walking. "Something wrong?"

Her stomach lurched and she felt as if she was going to be sick. The red hair had thrown her because three years ago during that father-daughter bike ride, Sally had been a brunette.

"Jill." Dan's voice seemed to come from a great distance. "Tell me what's wrong."

She focused on his face, noting that his forehead was crinkled with concern. Yet how could she tell him about Sally without explaining why remembering where she'd recognized the woman from was a problem?

She cleared her throat. "It's nothing."

"Are you sure? You look pale."

"I probably just need some water," she said. "It's hot outside today."

"Then let's get you some water." He took her elbow

and guided her through the resort to the gift shop in the lobby. He went straight to the cold beverages, opened the refrigerated compartment and handed her a bottle of water.

She opened the bottle and drank from it as he went to the cash register and paid. Her mind whirred as the cold liquid slid down her throat. She tried—and failed—to remember if Sally had been on more than the single ride, yet she did recall that Sally's father was an avid member of the Atlanta biking community.

Yet Sally had seemed satisfied that she recognized Jill from the Blue Haven. If Jill hadn't been talking about mountain biking as she and Dan passed the meeting room, she wouldn't have put the puzzle together. Sally might not, either.

"Thanks for the water," she told Dan when he rejoined her and they walked together out of the gift shop.

"Any time." He placed a hand at her back and lightly steered her toward the elevator, not giving her the option of taking the stairs as she usually did. He pressed the call button, then ran concerned eyes over her.

"Would you mind taking a shower in the other room so we can get on the road quicker?" she asked. Even though Sally Tomlin wasn't working the rest of the weekend, Jill was afraid she'd suddenly materialize.

"Sure," he said. "Are you feeling better?"

Jill arranged her mouth into a smile. She was over-reacting. Even if Sally remembered how she knew Jill and mentioned their meeting to her father, what were the chances that Sally's father would contact Jill's father?

Slim, Jill thought. Since Jill's father had married Arianne, he'd largely lost touch with his old life and his old friends.

"I'll be fine," Jill answered, praying she spoke the truth.

CHAPTER TWELVE

CHRIS FOLLOWED THE friskier of the two scampering pygmy goats around Dan's backyard, holding a leather collar and leash behind his back.

"Here, Bluebell," the boy cried out in a singsong voice.

Dan leaned back against a tall oak tree and crossed his feet at the ankles, settling in for a show.

"Here, girl. Come to Chris."

The little goat slowed down marginally. Chris pounced, brandishing the leash and lunging for the animal. Bluebell spurted forward. Chris missed the goat altogether, falling to his knees in the grass. Bluebell ran around the perimeter of the fence, playfully kicking up her hooves.

Dan hid a smile and called, "I don't think she's going to let you catch her."

Chris sprang to his feet, looking energized even though he'd been to a sleepover the night before where he said he got only a few hours of shut-eye. The boy didn't bother to wipe at the dirt and grass on his knees. "Bluebell doesn't understand I only want to take her for a walk."

Dan was about to point out it might be easier to catch Tinkerbell, the goat who had a week to go before its cast could be removed, then thought better of it. Even with the plaster on her leg, Tinkerbell wouldn't let herself be collared, either.

Chris chased Bluebell one more time around the yard, lunging and missing yet again. The boy finally trudged over to the back porch, his head bowed so his dark hair hung in his eyes. He set down the leash in defeat.

Both Bluebell and Tinkerbell came running to him when he walked back into the yard, nudging him playfully, the way they did when they wanted some love.

"Gol durned! Dag nab it!" Chris cried.

Dan chuckled, straightening from his position by the tree and joining the boy and the goats in the yard. "Is that what Mrs. Feldman says when she gets upset?"

Chris scratched Bluebell behind the ear and laughed when Tinkerbell tried to horn in on the action. "No. My dad. Usually at Falcons games."

The Falcons were the professional football franchise located in Atlanta. Considering that Chris had spent the first few years of his life in Georgia, it made sense that his father would have been an Atlanta fan.

"Have you been to any Falcons games?" he asked the boy.

"Dad takes me all the time." Chris attempted to keep both of the goats happy, scratching first one, then the other, laughing all the time. "He has season tickets."

"That must have been quite a drive," Dan remarked.

Chris kept playing with the goats, his attention only half on the conversation. "We don't drive. We take MARTA."

The things Chris was saying weren't adding up. If the boy had left Georgia as a baby or even a toddler, he wouldn't remember attending the football games. Dan must have misunderstood how old Chris was when he moved to South Carolina. Or maybe Chris and his father had gone to the games while visiting relatives in Atlanta.

Even as Dan worked out the logical explanation in his mind, something else didn't compute. Why had Chris spoken of his deceased father in the present tense?

"I want to get Dad a Falcons jersey for his birthday," the boy announced as the goats continued to compete for his favor.

Dan's whole body went still. "When's his birthday?"

"August thirtieth," Chris answered absently.

Bluebell put her two front hooves on Chris's chest in a desperate ploy for attention. Chris giggled wildly, stepped back so the goat had to put all four legs on the ground, then took off in a run. The goats dashed after him, as though the three of them were playing a game of tag.

Dan didn't crack a smile.

Either Chris had yet to process the fact that his father was dead or the man was alive.

His heart pounded so hard it felt as if it were trying to escape his chest, yet he told himself not to jump to the worst possible conclusion. Jill wasn't a liar. She might have asked him not to speak to Chris about his father because she knew her brother was in deep denial. Whatever the reason, he needed to figure out what was going on.

Jill had tonight off from the Blue Haven and was supposed to call him after she met Penelope Pollock and Sara Brenneman for an early dinner. The light was fading fast, signaling he should walk Chris home. With any luck, he'd arrive at Mrs. Feldman's house approximately when Jill did.

His timing turned out to be slightly off. That wasn't a problem for Mrs. Feldman. She shooed Chris upstairs to take a shower and invited Dan to sample a slice of apple pie while he waited. She insisted on heating the pie in the microwave and adding a dollop of French vanilla ice cream.

More convinced by the minute that Jill would have a logical explanation, Dan shelved his worries and concentrated on enjoying the dessert.

"This is the best apple pie I've eaten in my entire life," he exclaimed.

Mrs. Feldman chuckled with pleasure. "That's high praise. No wonder Jill is so charmed by you."

"Did Jill tell you that?" he asked, another heaping bite of pie balanced on his fork.

"She didn't have to tell me anything," Mrs. Feldman said. "I knew when I looked out the window and saw you kissing her that you curled her toes. Why, you're the first man she's given the time of day to since she moved here."

Dan set the forkful of pie back down on his plate. "Does she ever talk about her life before she moved here?"

"Can't say that she does," Mrs. Feldman said. "Why do you ask?"

Because he wanted confirmation that the things Jill had told him were true. A peeling sound pierced the apple-pie-scented air before he could respond. A phone, but not the old-fashioned country phone with the rotary dial suspended from the kitchen wall. This one was a plain black cell phone lying on the kitchen counter.

"That's Jill's phone." Mrs. Feldman let it ring. "She must have forgotten it."

The cell phone stopped ringing. An instant later, the wall phone started.

"It's probably the same person." Mrs. Feldman rose and shuffled over to the phone, lifting the receiver and greeting the caller.

She listened for a moment, then said, "No. I'm sorry, Chuck. Jill's cell phone's here, but she's not."

Chuck was Jill's boss at the Blue Haven. Dan hoped like hell he wasn't calling to get Jill to cover for someone at work tonight.

Mrs. Feldman grew quiet, her entire body freezing. Her right hand gripped the receiver tightly as she concentrated intently on what was being said. Finally she spoke. "That is strange. I'm sure Jill will appreciate you calling to tell her about it."

She nodded at whatever Chuck replied as she twisted the telephone cord.

"I'll let her know the minute she gets home," Mrs. Feldman promised. "And don't you worry about telling me her business. I couldn't love that girl any more if she was my own."

Mrs. Feldman finally replaced the receiver on the cradle but didn't head back to the table. The wrinkles on her face seemed to have deepened.

"Something's wrong," Dan said.

She stared at him. "You care about Jill, don't you?"

He didn't only care about Jill, he loved her.

The thought struck him with such force it left him momentarily speechless. When, he wondered, had that happened? The answer immediately presented itself.

He'd fallen in love with Jill this past weekend. Not when she'd stripped at the waterfall but the next morning in bed when she'd finally trusted him enough to start answering his questions.

"Yes," he said. "I care about her."

"Then I don't see any reason not to tell you. A man phoned the Blue Haven asking lots of questions about Jill. When her shifts were. Where she was living. Whether she had a boy with her."

As if a siren had gone off, the warning resonating inside Dan couldn't have been clearer.

"Chuck wouldn't tell him anything, not even whether Jill worked there," Mrs. Feldman continued. "He turned the tables and asked the man why he was calling. You know what the man did?"

Dan shook his head wordlessly.

"He hung up. Now, what do you make of that?"

Dan couldn't make sense of it. He did know one thing for certain, though. The woman he'd fallen in love with was keeping something from him, maybe even something bigger than his ex-fiancée had.

"FELICIA! CHRIS! I'M HOME," Jill called, her mind already racing ahead to her plans for the rest of the evening.

If she'd remembered her cell phone, she already would have called Dan and let him know she was available. Available. She giggled aloud at her most accurate choice of words. Where Dan Maguire was concerned, she was eminently available.

She walked over the hardwood of the foyer, the clap of her heels sounding unnaturally loud as she breathed in a scent she identified as apple pie. "Where is everybody?"

"In the kitchen," Felicia answered, the direction Jill was headed anyway.

"Wait till you try these leftovers I brought home." Jill talked as she walked, conscious of the seconds ticking by. The longer she lingered at home, the less time she'd have to spend with Dan. "It's chicken penne with gorgonzola and it's…"

She stopped short. Dan sat at the white kitchen table across from Felicia, a half-full glass of milk and an empty pie plate in front of him. With his dark hair and solid build he looked exceedingly masculine in her landlady's frilly country kitchen, calling to mind all the questions Penelope and Sara had asked over dinner about their developing relationship.

Jill had responded to only half of them, although she'd felt herself blushing too many times to count, which her friends had taken as confirmation of a hot romance.

"Dan!" She felt her mouth stretch in a wide smile. "I was just going to call you."

"I walked Chris home and had some pie while I waited for you," Dan said.

Although his words were light, his expression wasn't. Neither was Felicia's.

"Is everything okay?" Jill asked.

"Probably." Felicia twisted her hands as she answered. "It's just that Chuck called from the Blue Haven."

Jill groaned and walked to the refrigerator with the container of leftovers. "He wants me to come into work tonight, doesn't he?"

"No, no. That's not it," Felicia said. "He wanted to warn you a man called the bar asking questions about you."

Jill's breath snagged, and her heart felt as though it ground to a sudden halt. She regarded her landlady over the kitchen counter, aware that Dan was watching her closely. "What kind of questions?"

Felicia told her, confirming Jill's worst fears.

Her father's private eye had found her, possibly because of her chance encounter with Sally Tomlin. The reason hardly mattered now, though.

"Did Chuck tell him anything?" Jill asked sharply. Too sharply.

"No," Felicia said. "He wouldn't even say whether you worked there."

"Any idea who this guy is?" Dan asked, his gaze piercing.

She broke eye contact and opened the refrigerator door, fighting to mask her panic. The private eye knew she worked at the Blue Haven. She prayed the reason he hadn't paid the bar a personal visit was that he wasn't in Indigo Springs. He'd be here soon, though. It was only a matter of time until he showed up at Felicia's house.

Jill put the container of leftovers on a refrigerator shelf, shut the door and reached for a logical explanation. "I'm sure it's nothing to worry about. Guys at the bar get a little too friendly all the time. It was probably one of those."

"I don't think so, dear." Felicia was still wringing her hands. "Chuck said the man had a Southern accent and he didn't recognize his voice."

Jill mentally grasped for another reasonable story even as she processed the damning information that the caller was a Southerner. "Then it must've been somebody from one of my white-water trips."

She affixed a smile to her face, trying to figure out how much longer she dared stay in Indigo Springs.

Not days, she concluded. Hours.

"You need to be careful and pay attention to what's going on around you." Dan's tone was as serious as his expression.

Jill nodded, her throat thick. She was very well aware of what she had to do and how much it would hurt, not only herself but also the people she cared about.

"Where's Chris?" Jill asked.

"In his room," Felicia replied. "He said he was going to play video games, but it wouldn't surprise me if he's asleep. That sleepover last night tuckered him out."

She and Chris probably couldn't leave tonight, then. Chris was a heavy sleeper. He'd resist if she woke him in the middle of the night. He still slept with a night light, so she'd be able to pack his things, though. Then she needed to figure out where they were going.

A powerful wave of sadness washed over her. She and Chris were happy here in Indigo Springs. She didn't want to leave her friends, Felicia and the wonderful warmth of the house that had become a home.

Most of all, she didn't want to leave Dan.

"I'm tired, too." She avoided looking at him, afraid she wouldn't be able to keep the despair out of her eyes. She was about to cancel the plans they'd made to get together tonight, plans she'd never be able to reschedule. "I'm afraid it'd be best if I turned in early tonight."

"I need to talk to you about something first," Dan said firmly.

She disliked the note of seriousness in his voice. As much as she longed to spend more time with him, she couldn't risk it. She swallowed.

"Can't it wait until tomorrow?" she asked, fully expecting him to comply.

"No, it can't." He glanced toward the staircase that led to the second floor, then quieted his voice. "It's about Chris."

Felicia quickly took control of the situation, whispering, "Why don't you two go outside and talk on the porch where Chris won't hear you?"

Jill could hardly refuse. She fruitlessly wished that circumstances were different, that she was headed outside to steal a few private moments with her lover. The air was balmy and the porch swing spoke of romance and lazy summer nights. Jill avoided the swing, taking a seat in one of the wicker chairs. Dan sat down in the chair beside hers.

"What about Chris?" She hated herself for sounding abrupt, especially when she could see he was confused by her behavior. If she lingered with him on the wrap-around porch, though, the defenses she was trying hard to erect would tumble.

"He said your dad used to take him to Falcons games

and they lived close enough to the stadium to take public transportation," Dan said.

He waited, watching her carefully. She almost laughed at the irony. For years she'd been trying to get Chris to stop lying. It was the truth, however, that was causing her problems.

"I can see where that was confusing. I didn't live with my father growing up, but my brother did. They spent years in Atlanta." Jill hoped that was consistent with what she'd already told Dan. At this point, she was so rattled she couldn't be sure of anything.

Dan leaned forward, balancing his forearms on his thighs, his eyes boring into her. She heard an owl hoot, cicadas sing and the creak of his wicker chair.

"That's not all," he said. "Chris spoke of your father as if he were alive. He said he wanted to get him a Falcons jersey for his birthday."

She felt her palms grow damp. The cover story she'd guarded so carefully was crumbling like the topping on Felicia's apple cake.

"That's…troubling. I'll have to talk to Chris about that." Jill stood up, not able to bear discussing this with him any longer. Few things could be more painful than lying to a man she cared for so deeply. "Thanks for telling me."

She backed toward the front door, trying to convey that she wanted him to leave. "If that's all, I really am tired."

The only thing that moved were the muscles in his face, which formed a frown.

"What's going on with you, Jill?" he asked. "Things

aren't adding up. Your stories. That phone call. And now it seems like you can't wait to get rid of me."

She swallowed. "I told you. I'm tired."

He shook his head. "That's not it. We had plans for tonight. You gave the impression you were eager to be alone with me."

She'd said more than that during phone calls since their weekend together. She said she craved him. How could she credibly explain her about-face? Her stomach cramped until she felt as if she were going to be sick, because she realized there was only one solution.

"I changed my mind." Her voice cracked, but she forced herself to keep talking. "This is hard to say, but I don't want to see you anymore."

He looked as if she'd struck him. "You're dumping me?"

"Yes." She hated herself for sounding heartless even though it was the only way to get him to leave. She straightened her backbone and strove to make her voice more forceful. "I told you it wasn't a good time for me to be in a relationship."

He got to his feet, confusion stamped on his features. She doubted her ability to continue the charade if he touched her. She retreated farther, her back coming flush against the screen door.

She couldn't let the pain she was causing him sway her. She needed to think of Chris and his safety.

"I don't understand," he said. "What did I do?"

"You didn't do anything." The backs of her eyes burned. She willed herself not to cry. "Things will never work out between us. It's best to cut things off before we get any deeper. Can you understand that?"

He raised his chin and set his jaw, but not before she saw him flinch. The anguish that spread through her seemed to settle in her heart and fester.

"I understand perfectly," he said gruffly.

Then he turned and walked out of her life. She watched him go, with his hands shoved into his pockets and his back ramrod straight. She had an overwhelming urge to run after him, to beg him to forgive her, to tell him how much he meant to her.

She did none of those things.

Her eyes teared up. Determinedly she blinked the moisture away and walked into the house.

She had clothes to pack—and a brother to protect.

DAN FLOPPED OVER from his back to his side and glanced at the glowing red numbers on his bedside alarm clock—5:43 a.m. After tossing and turning for much of the night, he'd managed to fall asleep after all.

One of the bedroom shades wasn't pulled all the way down, revealing that the sky had barely begun to brighten. Now that he was awake, though, he wouldn't be able to sleep again.

He sat up in bed. His head felt fuzzy, his eyes gritty, his mouth dry. He braced himself for the sharp disappointment that had ravaged him last night. The edges had dulled, leaving him with something resembling a hangover.

He got out of bed, then methodically went about his morning routine. Once he was in the kitchen, he switched on the overhead light, took some orange juice from the refrigerator and slugged straight from the carton.

The click of canine toenails against the hardwood floor preceded Starsky's entrance. The dog trudged sleepily to Dan's side, then rubbed the side of his head against Dan's leg.

"You can tell I'm hurting, huh?" Dan reached down and scratched the dog behind his ear. "The thing is, I don't know what went wrong."

Hutch barked from the living room, then rushed into the kitchen, his tail wagging enthusiastically. The second dog dashed to the hook by the rear door where Dan kept the leashes, then ran back to Dan.

"A walk? Why not?" Dan had awakened early enough that he had time to kill before work, and the fresh air might clear his head even if it wouldn't heal his heart.

The morning haze hadn't yet worn off, causing the sky to appear indistinct. He held both leashes in one hand, letting the dogs set the pace while his mind drifted. The sun was a pale yellow blur rising above the horizon, the way it might look if viewed through a pair of glasses with the wrong prescription.

Dan's perspective on the breakup with Jill had been similarly hazy the night before. One minute everything had seemed fine. The next she'd gone out of her way to tell him in no uncertain terms it was over.

But why?

He'd viewed the situation emotionally the night before. Now he tried to consider it dispassionately.

It still didn't make sense.

He'd been caught unaware by Maggie, too. Yet in retrospect, Maggie had distanced herself from him with small steps. By the time she left, they hadn't had a meaningful conversation in ages. It had been more than a month since they'd had sex.

Dan and Jill had had sex—no, made love—three days ago. He'd had every expectation they would make love again last night. Jill hadn't grown cold until he mentioned that her brother thought their father was alive.

No, that wasn't quite accurate. She'd started acting differently when Mrs. Feldman told her about the phone call.

Those two things must be related. But how? In retrospect he should have come out and asked Jill point-blank if her father were alive. He'd intended to, but then she'd said they were through and he'd gotten sidetracked. Had she distracted him on purpose?

Starsky barked and put on a burst of speed, running to the end of the retractable leash and pulling. Hutch followed enthusiastically so that Dan had to keep a firm hold on both leashes.

While thinking about Jill, Dan had walked in the direction of Mrs. Feldman's house. There was little activity on the hilly block, with the cars that had been parked overnight on the street still in the same spots and the town just waking up.

He spotted a dark-haired woman up ahead, carrying something to her car. Jill. He let the dogs lead him closer, and it became clear she was toting duffel bags to a car that was already filled to overflowing. Bedding, a small television, Chris's video game system and the giant teddy bear he'd won in Hershey already occupied the backseat.

Jill was leaving town. Not at some distant point in the future. Now.

She stood stock-still as Starsky and Hutch pranced around her, her eyes locked with his, her ready smile absent. She wore traveling clothes: worn, comfortable jeans and a sky-blue T-shirt he'd seen in one of the local gift-shop windows. The saying on it read "I heart Indigo Springs."

"Starsky! Hutch! Sit!" His unyielding tone was one he seldom used with the dogs. They calmed down immediately.

Jill broke eye contact and proceeded to the car, setting down the bags on the road and opening the trunk. It, too, was nearly packed.

"What's going on, Jill?" Dan asked.

She put the bags into the trunk, then closed it. She seemed to be avoiding looking at him. "Isn't it obvious?"

"No," he said. "I knew you were thinking about leaving town, but you didn't say anything about leaving today."

"Goodbyes are hard." She still wouldn't meet his eyes. "I wanted to avoid them."

None of this added up. She was part of the community, with good friends, a landlady who loved her and two jobs. Just this past weekend, she'd rejoiced that her brother was finally making friends his own age and had told the Pocono Challenge organizers she'd lead a bike ride if they chose Indigo Springs as a finalist.

"Does this have something to do with the guy who called the bar? Are you in some kind of trouble?" He posed the questions he should have asked the night before.

She finally looked at him. He thought he read despair

on her face. A muscle twitched in her jaw. She opened her mouth, closed it, then said, "I need to get Chris."

She pivoted and walked away from him, getting halfway up the sidewalk before the front door of the house opened. Mrs. Feldman emerged wearing a housecoat and slippers. Her entire face seemed to sag.

"Dan." She perked up a little when she spotted him. "Thank goodness you're here. I've been trying to get Jill to change her mind about leaving for the past hour. Have you had any luck?"

Jill didn't give him a chance to respond. "I'm not going to change my mind, Felicia. I need to leave as soon as I get Chris."

"I came outside to tell you about Chris." Mrs. Feldman shuffled forward, stopping at the top of the porch. Hanging flower pots flanked her. "He just took off out the back door. He said something about saying goodbye to those goats."

Jill's shoulders visibly slumped. "I should have expected that."

"He's upset. He says he doesn't want to leave." Mrs. Feldman took a shuddering breath. "I don't want you to leave either."

"Thanks for telling me." Jill did nothing to console her landlady, cementing Dan's impression that something was seriously off. "I'll pick him up and leave from Dan's house, then."

"Oh, please don't do that!" Mrs. Feldman cried. She clutched at the porch railing, as though for support. "Chris left so suddenly I didn't have a chance to say goodbye. Please bring him back here before you go."

"I don't think—" Jill began.

Mrs. Feldman sniffled, and Jill didn't finish her sentence. Jill nodded. "I can do that."

"Thank you." Mrs. Feldman wiped under her eyes with the pads of her fingers, then nodded toward the house. Her voice wavered, as though she was struggling not to cry. "I'll be in the kitchen."

The landlady disappeared inside the house with Jill watching. Jill's shoulders seemed to shake before she squared them, turned back around and headed for the sidewalk that ran adjacent to the street. Dan was quicker than she was, stepping in front of her and blocking her path.

"Get out of my way, Dan." She didn't raise her head, but there was a definite quiver in her voice. He tipped up her chin. Moisture swam in her eyes.

"Not until you tell me what's really going on," he said.

CHAPTER THIRTEEN

JILL BLINKED AWAY her tears, bringing Dan's face into focus. His expression was both tender and determined.

The morning was going nothing like she'd planned. She and Chris were already supposed to be on the road, heading away from the town and the people they'd come to love.

She hadn't anticipated Felicia tearfully claiming her life wouldn't be the same without them, Chris stealing away to be with the pygmy goats or Dan showing up.

Most of all, she hadn't counted on this being the moment she realized she loved him.

The feeling had been coming on gradually since that barbecue with the Pollocks. It had crystallized over time as she'd watched his dealings with Chris and gotten to know him as a man of substance.

Yet she'd refused to put a name on her emotions. Admitting to herself that she loved Dan would have meant telling him the truth. For how could she love a man if she couldn't trust him with her deepest secrets?

"Tell me what's going on, Jill," he repeated, his fingers still touching her chin. There were smudges under his eyes, as though he hadn't gotten much sleep. Because of her, no doubt.

Thoughts swirled inside her head like leaves in the wind.

No matter how much she ached to explain her predicament, that would take time and she had a terrible sense her time was running out. The moment when she should have confided in Dan was already past.

"It's too late," she whispered.

He flinched as though she'd struck him. He dropped his hand from her cheek, his eyes grew hooded and he stepped back from her.

Blood roared in her ears, nearly obliterating the sounds of his dogs panting and an approaching car. She should say she was sorry, except she wouldn't be able to explain what she was apologizing for.

A car door opened and shut. Someone had parked along the curb and was walking toward them. She looked past Dan and gasped.

It was her father.

He looked older than when she'd last seen him, his hair considerably grayer, his posture not quite as erect. Unfamiliar lines bracketed his mouth and eyes.

"I found you, Jill." Her father had never been a volatile man, but anger vibrated from him. His voice shook. "It's over."

She'd had nightmares about this scenario. In those dark dreams she was always alone, a solitary woman determined to keep fighting for her brother. Now Dan positioned himself between Jill and her father, looming over the older man by a good five or six inches.

"Don't come any closer," he warned in a low, ominous voice.

Despair reached inside Jill and burrowed. Not only had she failed Chris, she was about to introduce Dan, a man who was ready to leap to her defense, to the father she'd claimed was dead.

"It's all right, Dan." She laid a hand on his arm and felt the tension in his coiled muscles. "This is Mark Jacobi. My father."

"Your father." He repeated the words without surprise, yet his head shook back and forth. Once again she couldn't look him in the eye, afraid of what she'd see.

"Who are you?" her father asked him.

Dan moved his arm, and she was forced to drop her hand. "Dan Maguire. I'm a...friend of your daughter's."

Her father's gaze flickered to the packed car. "A friend, huh? If you were a true friend, you wouldn't help her. You would have told her to give me back my son."

"I don't know what you're talking about," Dan said flatly.

"Jill took Chris without my permission." Her father stood just off the sidewalk, in the dewy grass. He didn't seem to notice his shoes were getting damp. "That was more than a year ago."

Jill dared not try to gauge Dan's reaction. She needed to keep her wits about her in case an opportunity presented itself to give her father the slip. "How did you find me?"

"Ralph Tomlin said his daughter ran into you. My P.I. made some calls and came up with this address last night. This morning I chartered a plane. I couldn't risk that you'd run again." Her father relayed the facts with what sounded like barely controlled fury, but Jill wasn't fooled. Stark pain shadowed his eyes.

"I never meant to hurt you, Daddy." Jill felt as though a vice was gripping her heart. "But I didn't have a choice. I couldn't leave Chris in the same house as Arianne."

"Chris lied about that!" her father cried. "Arianne never did anything to him."

"How would you know?" Jill retorted. "You have such a blind spot about her, you can't see anything clearly."

"Would someone tell me what's going on?" Dan still stood between them, closer to Jill than her father, his expression unreadable.

She tried to explain, but her father interrupted every time she said something negative about Arianne. Clearly his feelings about his third wife hadn't changed. Finally she gave up, unsure if she'd been able to convey to Dan the gravity of the situation.

"You can see that the story's preposterous." Her father took a step toward Felicia's house. "Where's my son? Is he in there?"

"No," Jill said while she desperately tried to figure out how to keep her father and brother apart. If the two of them crossed paths, she'd be unable to prevent her father from taking Chris back to Atlanta.

"Don't lie to me," her father warned. "I know Chris is living with you."

"I'm not lying," Jill said. "He's not inside the house. He's somewhere safe."

"I haven't called the cops because you're my daughter. But believe me, this time I will." He abruptly turned to Dan. "Do you want to see her go to jail?"

"Don't threaten her," Dan said in a low growl.

"Then *you* tell me where my son is," her father demanded.

Jill intercepted Dan's gaze, silently pleading with him to remain quiet. She thought of her ex-boyfriend Ray Williams, insisting he had an obligation to tell her father Jill's plans. She waited for Dan's response.

"Your son's somewhere safe." Dan repeated the same words she'd used. "If you want him back, you'll have to give your daughter some assurances."

It had been so long since Jill had had someone in her corner fighting for her that she almost wept with relief.

"What!" her father exclaimed. "That's not the way it works. I have the law on my side."

"Then let's sit down and talk. Your daughter wouldn't have done this without good reason. You owe it to your son to hear her out." Dan had no reason to believe in Jill, yet spoke with conviction.

"Why should I?" her father retorted. "Look, Social Services already investigated. They found nothing."

"They must have been wrong," Dan stated forcefully. "You could at least listen to Jill's reasons."

"I already know her reasons."

"Not until you let her talk without interrupting her, you don't," Dan said sternly, and she fell a little deeper in love with him. "Listen first, then tell your side of the story."

Her father said nothing for several long minutes, a muscle working in his jaw. "Okay," he finally said.

The pressure on Jill's chest lessened. There were no guarantees talking would work, but at least it was a start.

She tried to catch Dan's eyes, to convey how extremely grateful she was, but he wouldn't look at her.

The vice on her heart tightened again.

JILL'S FATHER WAS NO FOOL.

Before he entered Mrs. Feldman's house, he demanded assurances that his son wouldn't be whisked out of town while he was preoccupied. He listened in while Dan phoned Annie Whitmore and asked her to pick up Chris, then reiterated he'd call the cops if necessary.

"Thanks for the coffee and the muffins," Mark Jacobi told Mrs. Feldman once they were indoors. Dan sat at one end of the kitchen table, between father and daughter.

"Think nothing of it." The landlady hovered over them, her tears dried but her eyes red rimmed. She'd seemed as surprised as Dan to be introduced to Jill's father. He wondered if she'd also been under the impression that Mr. Jacobi was dead. "I'll be upstairs if you need me."

Nobody spoke until the sound of Mrs. Feldman's footsteps faded as she climbed the stairs. Even though the landlady must be brimming with curiosity, she hadn't asked questions.

Jill's father, however, was full of them.

"I keep asking myself how my own daughter could do something like this to me." Mr. Jacobi focused on Jill's solemn, worried face. "So make me understand."

The house smelled of coffee and the homemade blueberry muffins none of them had touched. Starsky and Hutch barked playfully in the backyard where Dan had left them. Mr. Jacobi hadn't blinked at Dan's continued presence, apparently believing Dan was in Jill's circle of trust.

Trust.

Dan's gut twisted at the irony intrinsic in the word. He'd wholeheartedly trusted Jill ever since they'd met, positive she was the opposite of his secretive ex-fiancée.

Yet Jill had lied to him, too.

Her father wasn't dead, her brother wasn't an orphan and she wasn't the woman she'd claimed to be.

"I never meant to hurt you, Daddy," Jill pleaded, sounding every inch a Southerner. Dan had once teasingly accused her of toning down her accent. Now he understood he'd been on the money. "I did what I had to do to protect Chris."

A muted buzzing noise sounded. Mr. Jacobi started, then patted his pocket where the outline of a cell phone was visible.

"I can look out for my own son." Mr. Jacobi put both hands on the table, the veins in them visible. "It's insulting for you to imply that I can't."

"How can you protect Chris if you won't accept there's something to protect him from?" Jill asked. "I know you don't believe Arianne abused Chris—"

"The social worker who came out to investigate didn't believe it, either," Mr. Jacobi repeated.

"The social worker said she couldn't prove abuse because Chris didn't have any marks or bruises," Jill rejoined. "That's not the same as saying he hadn't been abused."

Dan let them talk, trying to put together the puzzle

from the bits and pieces he'd learned. He knew Mr. Jacobi had married Arianne after Chris's mother died, yet didn't have a read on the woman. He did remember, however, that Arianne was the name of the bully Chris had told him about.

"Arianne never touched Chris," Mr. Jacobi stated forcefully.

"But she told him he was worthless!" Jill protested. "She said she wished he'd never been born. She locked him in a closet so nobody would know when she left him home alone."

"None of that happened." Mr. Jacobi's Adam's apple bobbed. "You know your brother has a problem with lying."

"He wouldn't lie about those things!" Jill said. "He wouldn't lie about Arianne threatening to kill him if he told anybody what she'd done!"

"That doesn't sound like something a child would make up," Dan interjected, figuring he'd been quiet long enough.

"Chris would do anything to break up me and Arianne," Mr. Jacobi said. "You've got to understand where he's coming from. He doesn't want anyone to take his mother's place."

"That's just ridiculous!" Jill cried.

"What's ridiculous are the accusations Chris made." Mr. Jacobi's mouth set in a stubborn line. "I never heard Arianne say any of those things to him."

"Now, I'm an outsider here," Dan interjected, painfully aware of that fact, "but it seems to me your wife would try to keep the abuse from you."

"What abuse? Why would she abuse him at all?" Mr.

Jacobi leaned forward and posed the questions that had been rattling around in Dan's mind.

"Let me tell you what I think," Jill said. "Chris hasn't talked about Arianne in months, but he said some things when we first left Atlanta."

So Jill was from Atlanta, after all. A shaft of pain shot through Dan at the verification that she'd lied about her hometown. He quashed it and concentrated on her story, for Chris's sake.

"Arianne told Chris she wouldn't be stuck home taking care of a snot-nosed brat when she could be out enjoying herself," Jill continued. "I think Chris interfered with the lifestyle she wanted to live."

"You're grabbing at straws," Mr. Jacobi said. "Arianne knew when she married me I had a son."

"She probably thought you'd hire a nanny," Jill said.

"Chris had enough nannies after his mother died. He didn't need another one. I told Arianne that up front and she was fine with it."

"Except she might not have been," Jill said. "Think about it, Daddy. You're a good catch. Since you married Arianne, you bought a fancier car, moved into a bigger house and joined a country club."

"What are you driving at?"

"Arianne suggested all of those things. Maybe she didn't realize how much a child would cramp her style."

"You don't know what you're talking about." Mr. Jacobi shook his head back and forth. "You hardly know Arianne. She loves me."

"How well do *you* know her?" Jill countered. "You

said she wasn't from Atlanta. How do you know anything she's told you about herself is true?"

"Jill has a point. Not everyone's truthful." Dan's eyes touched on Jill. She looked away. "For your son's sake, why not have somebody look into her background?"

"I don't have to listen to this," Mr. Jacobi said, and Dan could almost picture a steel door slamming shut. "Arianne is my wife!"

"And Chris is your son!" Jill countered. "I know you love him. So why don't you do what's best for him?"

"You think believing his lies about his stepmother is what's best for him? It's clear Chris needs counseling and I'll get it for him," he said. "But I'm through talking. I want my son. I demand you take me to him."

His phone buzzed again. He took it out of his pocket with an impatient jerk of his hand, checked the small screen and frowned. "I need to get this."

He excused himself, then went to the back porch to take the call, leaving Dan and Jill alone.

"He's not listening to me." Jill turned to Dan, her eyes huge and beseeching. "What am I going to do?"

Dan had been giving that very question copious thought. Despite how he felt about the lies she'd told him, his entire focus was on helping her do what was best for Chris. "Running away isn't an option. I believe your father would call the police."

"Me, too," she said miserably, "but I can't have my father take Chris back to Atlanta, either."

"You could if you talked him into letting you stay in the house with them," Dan said. "That way, you can make sure Chris is safe. In the meantime, hire Sara Brenneman to see if you have any legal recourse. Lawyers know who the reputable private eyes are. She can refer you to one who can check out Arianne's background."

"That makes perfect sense." She reached across the table and laid a hand on his, her gaze soft. "You've been so great, Dan. I don't know how I'd get through this without you."

He slipped his hand out from under hers. "I'm doing it for Chris."

Her brows drew together, her expression pained. Her lips parted, but before she could say anything the door opened and Mr. Jacobi walked back into the kitchen. His complexion had lost color, and he looked as though he'd aged ten years.

"That was Arianne." He spoke in a monotone, his gaze unfocused. "She's leaving me and filing for divorce."

"I don't understand." Jill got up from the table and went to stand by her father. "I thought everything was fine between you."

"She's been having an affair." Mr. Jacobi swallowed, and his chin shook slightly. "I even know the guy—this pretentious jerk who's always at the country club. She says they're in love."

"Is he married, too?" Jill asked.

"Divorced. No kids. And about ten years younger than me." Mr. Jacobi recited the facts in a monotone. "Arianne says he's a better fit for her than I am."

Jill looked as stunned as her father, even though the comments her father relayed seemed to confirm she'd been on the mark about Arianne. Dan couldn't help thinking, however, that there was another chapter of the story to be written.

"Take a few minutes to yourself, Daddy," Jill said gently. Dan was struck at how quickly she'd gone from protective of her brother to supportive of her father. "I'll go to the Whitmores' house and bring Chris back here."

Mr. Jacobi nodded, then sank into one of the kitchen chairs. Despite the mistakes he'd made, Dan felt sorry for the man. He knew what it felt like to be blindsided by a woman.

The fog had burned off and the sun struggled to peek from behind the clouds when Dan walked with Jill onto the porch. She clutched at the railing the same way Felicia Feldman had earlier that morning.

"I can't believe that just happened," she said. "For so long, I've been terrified my father would find us. I never considered Arianne didn't want Chris back and that being found could be the best thing for Chris."

"That remains to be seen," Dan said. "Your father has a lot of making up to do with your brother."

"Don't I know it," Jill said. "Chris is too young to understand how vulnerable a man in love can be."

Dan's gut clenched.

"What bothers me," Jill continued, "is that Arianne is going to get away with what she did to my brother."

"It might still be worth a shot to have someone look into her background," Dan suggested. "It probably won't help Chris, but it can't hurt to have more information about Arianne. Maybe one day you'll need it."

"I'll do that." Jill let go of the porch railing, the decision to do something proactive seeming to fortify her. "I can't thank you enough for today."

"I was glad to help," he said.

"Let me ask you something." She watched him carefully. "Why did you believe I was doing the right thing for Chris? Not once did you question that."

He shrugged, not sure he could put his reasons into words, uncertain whether he even understood them. "I just did."

"I should go get Chris," Jill said. Her chest heaved up and down in a heavy sigh. She seemed to have difficulty getting the next words out. "Will you come with me?"

He shook his head. "This doesn't involve me anymore."

"I'd like it to involve you." She gazed at him with huge, pleading eyes. "You must know I didn't mean what I said last night. I don't want to break up with you."

"You haven't meant a lot of things you said." He kept his hands shoved into his pockets, annoyed with himself that even now he wanted to reach for her. "You've been lying to me pretty much since we met."

"Because I had to," she said. "I wanted to tell you about Chris, but I've been burned before. I couldn't risk it."

Pain sliced through him. "You actually thought I'd betray you to your father?"

She shook her head miserably. "I was confused. I had doubts, but now—"

He didn't let her finish. "I understand you couldn't bring yourself to trust me. I even accept it. Now I'm asking you to accept that I can't trust you. Not anymore."

"Would it matter if I said I was sorry?" Her voice shook. "Because I am sorry. I didn't think I had any choice but to lie."

He wasn't aware it was possible for a heart to physically hurt until just then. "There's always a choice."

He moved away from her, feeling as though he were wading through quicksand. His throat felt thick and his eyes moist. It seemed prophetic that her car was already packed, because this was the moment that felt like goodbye.

CHAPTER FOURTEEN

"ARE YOU READY YET, DAD?" Chris Jacobi paced the cool marble tile of his father's house in Atlanta two weeks later, stopping periodically to bounce on the balls of his feet.

Jill thought the excitement radiating from her brother made it seem as if his whole body was vibrating.

"Give me a minute, son." Mark Jacobi's tone was indulgent. "Your sister needs to talk to me first."

"We gotta get to the animal shelter before it closes!" Chris said.

"It's not even one o'clock, Chris," Jill pointed out, hiding a smile. "You've got plenty of time to get there."

Chris pursed his lips, frowned, then said. "I'll go wait by the car."

He dashed away from where Jill and her father sat on tall stools at the granite breakfast bar in a kitchen as spacious as some small houses. The sound of his footsteps thundered over the tile, followed by the front door slamming.

"Chris thinks waiting by the car will speed you up," Jill told him.

"I remember," her father said, a simple phrase that conveyed a world of meaning. Jill and Chris had left Indigo Springs with their father the day after he tracked them down. Since then, he'd been getting reacquainted with his son.

"It's a great idea to get him a pet," Jill said. "He had a hard time leaving those pygmy goats behind."

"I would have let him bring the goats with him if it hadn't been for the zoning ordinance," her father said. "I want Chris to be happy here."

"I know, Daddy." Jill could attest firsthand that he was trying his best to repair the damage to his relationship with his son. She'd taken Dan's advice and was temporarily living at the Atlanta house to help ease the transition for Chris.

Now that Arianne was no longer in the picture, with the help of counseling the boy was rebounding surprisingly well.

Jill wasn't faring as favorably. Every day she thought about the mistakes she'd made with Dan. No matter how much it pained her, she understood why he could never trust her again.

After all, her major mistake had been not trusting him.

"What did you want to talk to me about?" he asked.

"Arianne." She noticed his muscles tense, as though he was preparing to take a punch to the gut. "That private detective I hired called with more news."

He said nothing, simply waiting for her to continue, a marked contrast to his anger the first time she'd brought up the P.I. Much had happened since he'd claimed she had nerve to hire someone to probe into his wife's background without his permission.

Her father had found out Arianne had emptied their

joint accounts, and the P.I. discovered another state had a violation-of-probation warrant against her. It turned out Arianne had run up thousands of dollars on an ex-boyfriend's credit card, and he'd pressed charges. A judge had sentenced her to a fine, community service and one year of supervised probation. She'd fled the state a month later.

"That warrant caught up with her," Jill said. "She's looking at a mandatory jail sentence for violating probation."

"I know," her father said. "Arianne called and asked if I could hire a good lawyer to get her off."

Jill's breath caught. "What about the man she left you for? Why wouldn't *he* get her a lawyer?"

"Apparently he's not as in love with her as she thought."

"What did you say?" Jill asked.

"I said she could hire her own lawyer with the money she stole from my accounts." He winced. "Then she swore at me and hung up."

He spoke like a man whose heart had been broken.

"I'm sorry, Daddy," she said.

"I'm sorry I was such a fool." He wet his lips and took a deep breath before asking, "You really believe she did those things to Chris?"

"I really do," Jill said. "I don't think she had anything against him in particular. I just think the only person who matters in Arianne's life is Arianne."

Her father's eyes watered. "Why couldn't I see that?"

"Because you were in love," she said. "It's hard to see things clearly when you're in love."

Jill hadn't recognized a good man worthy of her trust. The ache of her regret intensified.

"Have you heard from Dan Maguire since we got back to Atlanta?" her father asked.

Jill didn't bother to try to convince him that she didn't equate Dan with love. She was through lying.

"He called Chris to tell him Tinkerbell's cast was off and he could come visit the goats any time. He didn't ask to speak to me." The admission hurt. "I lied to him about too many things. It's over between us."

"Maybe if you went back to Indigo Springs, you could start it up again," her father said. "The people in our family make good on their second chances. Just watch me."

She leaned forward and kissed him on the cheek, feeling closer to him than she had in years.

"You better go, Daddy," she said. "Chris is waiting."

He stood, planted a soft kiss on the top of her head and went to join his son. Only when he was gone did Jill draw in a shuddering breath.

She couldn't delay making a decision about her future much longer. Chris started back to school on Monday, and it had become increasingly clear that father and son would do just fine without her.

Her father's suggestion that she return to Indigo Springs had struck a nerve. Both her employers would welcome her back, as would Felicia. Without Chris to take care of, Jill could cut down on her work hours and even run for borough council.

Or she could try to get her old job back at the bike shop. She'd be close to family and wouldn't come into constant contact with Dan and her regrets over what might have been.

Then again, she didn't have to be in Indigo Springs to experience regret. If she'd handled her relationship with Dan differently, right now she'd be with him at his cousin's wedding in Ohio.

She abruptly got to her feet, went to the guest bedroom she was using and changed into a one-piece bathing suit. Swimming laps in her father's backyard pool might help crystallize her thoughts.

Forty-five minutes later, her only coherent thought was that she was tired.

She stopped swimming and leaned her head back in the water, closing her eyes and letting her body float. She couldn't hear anything except the muted sound of the water cascading down the stones artfully arranged in one corner of the pool area to resemble a waterfall. When she opened her eyes again, she saw a mirage. Dan stood beside the shallow end of the pool, looking tall and handsome and not quite real.

With no clouds in the sky, the sun was almost blindingly bright. She blinked a few times to clear the vision, but it persisted. He wore a short-sleeved shirt and khakis instead of the shorts in which her dream self would have dressed him. She righted herself so she was no longer floating but treading water. The man beside the pool, incredibly, was real.

"I let myself in through the gate when no one answered the doorbell," Dan called to her. "I hope you don't mind."

Wordlessly she shook her head, her arms and legs

working in tandem to keep her body afloat, her brain not working at all.

"Could you come out of the pool?" he asked. "It's a little hard to talk to you from here."

She swam to the ladder, feeling as though she was in a trance, and pulled herself out of the pool, water sluicing down her body. He greeted her with the towel she'd flung over the fence. She took it, wrapping it around her body, her eyes never leaving his face.

"Why aren't you at your cousin's wedding?" she asked, although that wasn't the question paramount in her mind. What was he doing *here?*

"I was in Ohio last night. Not at the wedding, at the rehearsal dinner. That's what I wanted to tell you about." He nodded to the big umbrella at the corner of the deck. "Can we get out of the sun?"

"Sure." She preceded him, taking one of the chairs underneath the circle of shade, trying to wrap her mind around the fact that Dan was in Atlanta with her.

He sat down at an angle to her. "Any news on Arianne?"

She filled him in as quickly as she could. He listened intently, nodding in all the right places, seemingly in no hurry to get off the subject. As soon as she finished, she blurted out, "You're killing me here, Dan. What about the rehearsal dinner?"

He smiled. "I did mention that, didn't I?"

"Yes," she said. "Now tell me what happened."

"Maggie was there," he explained, his expression suddenly serious. "It was the first time I'd talked to her since she left me. I finally asked her why she did it. Know what she said?"

Jill shook her head.

"She told me she left because things had been wrong between us for a long time. And that she thought I must have felt it, too. Maybe I had—I'm not sure."

Her pulse was suddenly racing. "Why are you telling me this?"

He reached across the table and took her hand, running his thumb lightly over her palm. "Remember when you asked why I believed you were doing the right thing for Chris? I finally figured it out. It's because I believe in *you*."

Her heart sped up, afraid she was mistaken about what she was hearing. "But...but I lied to you. I didn't trust you with the truth about Chris."

"I have some trust issues of my own," he said. "I should have trusted you were doing what you thought was best for your brother. More than that, I should have trusted my instincts."

She held her breath.

"What I'm trying to say is you're the one for me. I love you, Jill."

Her throat clogged. All she could do was stare at him.

He sighed. "I understand your feelings about me have changed. All I'm asking is that you give me another chance."

When she still didn't respond, he continued, "If you stay in Atlanta, I won't give up. I'll come see you every chance I get. If you'll let me, that is."

She put up a hand. "Dan, stop. The reason I'm not saying anything is because I'm about to cry."

He scooted his chair closer to her, his deep voice growing lower. "Why are you going to cry?"

She felt a fat tear drip down her cheek. "Because I love you, too."

She wasn't sure how it happened or who reached for whom, but suddenly she was in his arms, laughing and crying and kissing him.

"The only thing that would make this any better," he said when they came up for air, "is if you were coming back to Indigo Springs with me."

She thought of all that was waiting in her beautiful adopted town. Friends who cared about her. A landlady who treated her like a granddaughter. And the opportunity to build a life with the man she loved.

"Just try to stop me," she said.

EPILOGUE

Two months later

EERIE MUSIC DRIFTED through the night sky, sending a delicious thrill through Jill. The buzz of conversation from the crowd gathered in Whitmore Park for the first annual Halloween Lighting Ceremony grew louder.

"I'm *frightfully* afraid this ceremony will be a bust," Jill remarked to Dan. She swiped back some of the hair from her blond seventies wig and tried to adjust the badge, poking through to her chest.

"I don't know about that." Dan didn't seem to be experiencing any discomfort from his black wig and badge. He even moved well in his tight, flared jeans. "I think in Indigo Springs all things are possible."

One of his arms gathered her close against the side opposite to where his toy gun hung from his plastic holster.

"I know what you mean." Jill's gaze touched on their friends Annie and Ryan Whitmore, who it seemed hadn't stopped smiling since the teenage daughter they'd given up for adoption at birth had come to live with them. Annie and Ryan were watching Lindsey try to get Toby Bradford to come to her.

Two-year-old Toby tottered forward inch by inch, hampered by the oversize web feet attached to his green-

and-orange body suit. A matching hood with huge fake eyes completed the look.

"Toby makes an adorable frog," Sara Brenneman remarked to Kelly Bradford, Toby's adoptive mother.

"Oh, good. Chase said nobody would guess frog." Kelly turned to her husband with the sweetest I-told-you-so look Jill had ever seen. "I layered so many clothes under his costume for warmth, Chase said he looked like a dinosaur."

"I knew what Toby was right off the bat," Sara said. "But what the heck are Jill and Dan supposed to be? And why are they wearing sunglasses at night?"

"I was wondering why they're the only adults in costume." Michael Donahue stood behind Sara, his arms encircling his wife.

"It's two days before Halloween. We figured everyone would come in costume," Jill said. "I've got to admit, though, that our getups are a little obscure."

"They are not!" Dan tapped his police badge and gestured to Jill's. "These are the biggest clues. We're Starsky and Hutch."

"Your dogs?" Sara teased. "Then those are really bad costumes."

"Ha ha. Starsky and Hutch were TV cops from the seventies," Dan answered. "I have all the shows on DVD. After I get through making Jill watch them, Sara, you can borrow them."

"Thanks, but no thanks," Sara said. "I'm not watching any shoot-'em-up shows. Babies in the womb can hear what's going on outside, you know."

"Sara's been reading a lot of books for expectant

mothers." Michael rested his hands on Sara's stomach. At two months pregnant, she hadn't begun to show.

"I admit. I'm baby challenged." Sara glanced over her shoulder at her smiling husband. "I'm going to need lots of advice. Good thing I've got Kelly and Laurie."

"Where is Laurie anyway?" Dan looked around. "I don't see Kenny, either."

"Laurie would never bring little Miranda out in the cold," Jill said, referring to the couple's newborn daughter. "And Kenny wouldn't come without his family."

"Sierra wanted to be here, too, but she and Ben had to work." Ryan referred to his sister, who'd stunned everyone by moving to Pittsburgh with her investigative-reporter boyfriend, Ben Nash. "She got hired at Magee-Womens Hospital in Pittsburgh as an internist. She and Ben are going to visit here over Thanksgiving, I think to announce their engagement."

"That's great!" Penelope Pollock exclaimed. She and Johnny had joined the group of friends without Jill noticing. Jill couldn't miss Penelope now as the other woman sidled up to her. "Speaking of engagements, what's taking you two so long?"

"Penelope!" Johnny uttered a familiar admonishment.

"What?" Penelope flipped her orange scarf over her shoulder and balanced her hands on her black coat. "Jill and Dan might not even be together if not for me. So why can't I ask?"

"Because..." Johnny started to explain, then stopped and put an arm around his wife. "Never mind."

"So?" Penelope asked, eyes speculative as she turned

her attention once again to Jill and Dan. "Did you get her a ring yet, Dan?"

Jill couldn't help it. Her pulse quickened as she waited for his answer.

"Like I'd tell you first," Dan said, his tone playful.

"May I have your attention." Charlie Bradford's voice reverberated over a microphone, quieting the murmuring of the crowd. He stood with the seven members of the borough council flanking him. Jill took off her sunglasses to see Charlie better. He wore a reddish over-the-head costume with a yellow streak down the center. The sides of the outfit resembled an open bun.

"He's a hot dog!" Jill said with a smile.

"In more ways than one," Dan rejoined, grinning. He'd also removed his sunglasses, but his wig and badge were in place. "And he's saved us from being the only adults dressed for Halloween."

"First of all, I'd like to welcome everybody to our in-augural event, which is one of my initiatives as mayor," Charlie began.

"You go, hot dog!" Chase put his fingers in the sides of his mouth and whistled approval for his father. Laughter and applause rolled through the audience.

"If you get elected to the council, you'll be up there next year," Dan whispered in Jill's ear, sending warmth shooting through her. She was at the end of a short, intense campaign for a council seat.

"We can hope." She smiled at him, marveling that he could make her pulse quicken even dressed as a corny TV cop.

"Teresa." Charlie Bradford nodded to his wife. "Will you do the honors?"

Teresa threw a switch and the scaffolding beside her lit up. Jack-o'-lanterns of all sizes and carvings glowed in the night. There must have been two hundred of them, arranged in ten or more perpendicular rows, stacked one on top of the other. A pumpkin wall, Charlie had called it when he sent out the word to members of the community for contributions.

A group of schoolchildren, all in costume, started to sing a song about a pumpkin patch.

Jill had a fleeting thought of her father's surprising news that Chris was the star of his elementary school choir. Her father said that discovering he had a talent for singing was doing wonders for her brother's confidence.

"Let's get away from this crowd," Dan whispered directly into her ear, grabbing her hand.

Jill didn't need to be asked twice. She let Dan lead her away from where everyone was gathered, trusting he knew where he was going even though he headed deeper into the park.

He stopped in a secluded spot that was still in the glow of the jack-o'-lanterns. Jill looked up at him questioningly.

"I've got something to ask you," he said even though she hadn't said anything. More and more lately, they'd been communicating without words. "Except I'd rather do it when we're not wearing these getups."

"Done." She took off the disguise and shook out her hair. He did the same, and she was struck by the notion that they made a better team than their characters. "But whatever it is, I'll probably say yes."

"Good to hear." He reached into his pocket, withdrew

a black velvet box and snapped it open. A gleaming orange sapphire stone flanked by diamonds winked up at her. A Halloween color that would forever remind her of this magical moment. "Because I'm asking you to marry me."

"Yes!" she cried, flinging her arms around his neck.

He laughed. "You don't need to think about it?"

"What's to think about?" she said. "I love you."

"That means I was right," he said. "In Indigo Springs, anything *is* possible."

Then he kissed her in the glow of the pumpkin wall, with the promise of their future as bright as the celebratory lights.

* * * * *

COMING NEXT MONTH

Available November 9, 2010

LARGER-PRINT BOOKS!
GET 2 FREE LARGER-PRINT NOVELS PLUS
2 FREE GIFTS!

◆ HARLEQUIN®

Super Romance

Exciting, emotional, unexpected!

*See below for a sneak peek from
our inspirational line, Love Inspired® Suspense*

*Enjoy this heart-stopping excerpt from
RUNNING BLIND
by top author Shirlee McCoy,
available November 2010!*

*The mission trip to Mexico was supposed to be an
adventure. But the thrill turns sour when Jenna Dougherty
and her roommate Magdalena are kidnapped.*

"It's okay. I'm here to help." The voice was as deep as the
darkness, but Jenna Dougherty didn't believe the lie. She
could do nothing but lie still as hands slid down her arms,
felt the rope around her wrists.

"I'm going to use a knife to cut you free, Jenna. Hold
still."

The cold blade of a knife pressed close to her head before
her gag fell away.

"I—" she started, but her mouth was dry, and she could
do nothing but suck in air.

"Shhh. Whatever needs to be said can be said when
we're out of here." Nick spoke quietly, his hand gentle on
her cheek. There and gone as he sliced through the ropes on
her wrists and ankles.

He pulled her upright. "Come on. We may be on
borrowed time."

"I can't leave my friend," Jenna rasped out.

"There's no one here. Just us."

"She has to be here." Jenna took a step away.

"There's no one here. Let's go before that changes."

"It's dark. Maybe if we find a light…"

"What did you say?"

"We need to turn on the light. I can't leave until I know that—"

"What can you see, Jenna?"

"Nothing."

"No shadows? No light?"

"No."

"It's broad daylight. There's light spilling in from the window I climbed in through. You can't see it?"

She went cold at his words.

"I can't see anything."

"You've got a nasty bruise on your forehead. Maybe that has something to do with it." His fingers traced the tender flesh on her forehead.

"It doesn't matter *how* it happened. I'm blind!"

Can Nick help Jenna find her friend or will chasing this trail have Jenna running blindly again into danger?

Find out in RUNNING BLIND, available in November 2010 only from Love Inspired Suspense.

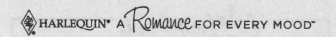

HARLEQUIN
Super Romance

Celebrate the Christmas season with
New York Times *bestselling author*

Brenda Novak

and fan favorites

Kathleen O'Brien

and

Karina Bliss

A young woman in search of a home…

A prodigal son's return…

A real-life Grinch transformed
by the magic of Christmas…

Curl up in front of the fire with
this joyous and uplifting anthology
that celebrates the true meaning
of Christmas.

Look for
THAT CHRISTMAS FEELING
available November
wherever books are sold.

"Don't threaten her," Dan said in a low growl.